Something is wrong
Morgan Creek.

A farmer goes missing after a blue in the pub. A teenage couple fail to show up for work. When Patrick and Sheila McDonough investigate, they discover the missing persons list is growing. Before they realise what's happening, the residents of the remote town find themselves in a fight for their lives against a foe they would never have suspected.

And the dry red earth will run with blood.

PRAISE FOR THE ROO

"…all I can say is …wow! Yes it's a bizarre concept, and of course there's a grindhouse feel to it. Lots of macabre violence and insanity, but at the core this book is about the people, not the crazy Roo, and deals with some heavy emotional issues. It's at times heartbreaking, terrifying and even hilarious. Alan has written a unique novella that will no doubt stay with you long after you've read it! You're in for a ride." – *Michael Evan,* **Fantasy Focus**

PRAISE FOR ALAN BAXTER

"Alan Baxter is an accomplished storyteller who ably evokes magic and menace." – *Laird Barron, author of* **Swift to Chase**.

"Baxter delivers the horror goods." – *Paul Tremblay, author of* **The Cabin at the End of the World**

"Step into the ring with Alan Baxter, I dare you. He writes with the grace, precision, and swift brutality of a prizefighter." – *Christopher Golden, New York Times bestselling author of* **Ararat** *and* **The Pandora Room**

"Alan Baxter delivers a heady mix of magic, monsters and bloody fights to the death. Nobody does kick-ass brutality like Baxter." – *Greig Beck, Internationally bestselling author*

"Alan Baxter's fiction is dark, disturbing, hard-hitting and heart-breakingly honest. He reflects on worlds known and unknown with compassion, and demonstrates an almost second-sight into human behaviour." — *Kaaron Warren, Shirley Jackson Award-winner and author of* **The Grief Hole**

"…if Stephen King and Jim Butcher ever had a love child then it would be Alan Baxter." – **Smash Dragons**

"Baxter draws you along a knife's edge of tension from the first page to the last, leaving your heart thumping and sweat on your brow." – **Midwest Book Review**

THE ROO

Alan Baxter

THE ROO

ISBN-13: 978-0-9805782-6-3
ISBN-10: 0-9805782-6-3

First Trade Paperback Edition - March 2020
Copyright © 2020 Alan Baxter

Cover Design © 2020 Elderlemon Design
Edited by Amanda J Spedding
Internal layout by David Wood

Alan Baxter
www.warriorscribe.com

For Leena
Thanks for your Strine!

FOREWORD

Or

A Killer Kangaroo Story? Are You Serious, Baxter?

This all started with a ridiculous situation on Twitter. There was a news article going around with the headline: 'Australian Town Terrorised By Muscular Kangaroo Attacking People And Eating Gardens'. You'll find it by searching for that sentence online. A more Australian story is hard to find.

When author Charles R Rutledge responded that it sounded "like something Zebra Books would have published back in the day", Kealan Patrick Burke (superb author and excellent cover designer) mocked up a brilliant old school horror novel cover in response. Several of us started joking about how a cover that cool really should be on an actual book. One thing led to another, and as I was the Aussie in the conversation, people started saying I should write it. And honestly, the cover had inspired me. I thought it would be a really fun creature feature, so I asked Kealan if I could have the cover were I to write a killer roo story. He said yes, but he wanted to polish it up, rather than the five-minute mock-up he'd done originally as a joke. So that's what he did. And enough people bugged me that I agreed to write it.

So here it is. I hope you enjoy it. The cover of the book in your hands is Kealan's amazing work in response to Charles's comment, that started the whole thing. I know you'll enjoy that amazing piece of art.

In keeping with the theme, I've shamelessly written this book to be as ocker as the outback. There are words and phrases herein that will no doubt confuse non-Aussies. So there's a (limited and certainly not exhaustive) glossary of Australian slang and terminology in the back. You might need to look up some translations. If you're not too familiar with the anatomy of kangaroos, may I also suggest you Google 'kangaroo feet' before you start reading. Seriously, you might think you know, but have another look. They're insane.

Almost every main character in this story is named after someone on Twitter who goaded and cajoled until I caved and agreed to write it. But I just used their names – the characters are most definitely not based on those people.

This is the kind of thing that happens when horror writers and reviewers are dicking around when they should be working.

Twitter: More dangerous than a killer kangaroo.

1

John Lynch stepped out of the George Hotel and spat blood into the red dirt gathered in the deep stone kerb. He didn't stagger, no sir. Sure, he was a few beers deep, but he wasn't drunk. He certainly wasn't the "aggro pissed bastard" Patrick McDonough had accused him of being, which led to pushing and shoving, which led to fists flying, and subsequently to John leaving the pub with blood in his mouth. Pat McDonough had blood of his own to spit out, too. No clear victor, unless you counted John's eviction. So Pat had knocked John onto his arse, that wasn't a victory. As John got back to his feet, Kealan Burke had yelled from behind the bar, threatened to come around the front with his cricket bat and bust skulls if John didn't fuck off out and not come back. Kealan always sided with Pat. But in a town of only four hundred people and a single pub, of course John would be back. The next day probably. The whole thing would blow over like these things always did. Maybe it was time to be getting home anyway, there was a lot of work to be done on the farm, most of it on his own these days.

He sniffed, spat again, winced. His cheek was coppery mince against his teeth where McDonough's gnarly old knuckles had landed. That was going to be sore for a few days. That arsehole. Pat wasn't a big man, certainly a lot smaller than John himself, but Pat was wiry and tough. Surprisingly strong, it turned out.

John looked left and right, watched a cloud of moths swarming around the streetlight outside the small real estate agents' office opposite for moment.

He glanced back at the pub, then said, "Fuck yas all" and strolled off along the footpath of Morgan Creek's one main street. The creek after which the town was named was a dry rocky scar in the landscape some kilometre or so north of him.

He blew air out. It was still hotter than a shearer's armpit even at nearly 11pm. And so dry the trees were chasing the dogs. Rain seemed like the memory of a dream. As he left the pool of streetlight, stars glittering in a blanket above, providing enough illumination to see by, John strolled towards the last shop, Carol's Café. Most of the folk in town would get lunch there at least a couple of times week. After that the pavement ran out and it was red dirt and scrubby paddocks for as far as a car could go on a tank of petrol, the city a virtual myth in the distance. John had been to the city a few times, but he didn't care for it. Weird fucken people inhabited cities.

John's farmstead was a good thirty-minute walk, and that was considered to be still in town by most, but he had his ute parked about a hundred metres down the road, pulled up on the dirt. Steve Gomzi, the town's one cop who didn't even live anywhere nearby, ignored drink driving as long as they parked outside the main street. Country law far more lax than elsewhere. Another benefit of not being anywhere near the city. No one could be expected to make those long walks, after all. Designated driver was city folk bullshit. As John strolled past Carol's, a large silhouette stepped out of the shadows on the far side.

"Come to have another go, McDonough, ya bastard?" His face ached. "Go root yer fucken boot, mate, I'm over it."

The shape shifted uncannily and moved further into the street, a leaning forward, then two oversized legs lifting and landing with a thud, ochre dust clouding.

"Fucken hell," John breathed. "That's the biggest fucken roo I ever saw." He giggled, maybe a little more drunk than he had first allowed. "Go on, Skip!" he shouted. "Go on, fuck off!"

The roo turned to face him. Its chest was twice as broad as John's and he was a big man. Deeply muscled under its red fur, its shoulders rounded balls of thick meat, even its biceps put John's own to shame. It leaned forward, and flexed, like a parody of Mr Universe. Or maybe not a parody, the thing's musculature enough to make John feel inadequate, despite a hard life of heavy farm work.

The roo's mouth opened with a soft grunt. Its eyes glowed fiery orange. John startled, realised it wasn't reflected streetlight, but the beast's eyes had seemed to ignite with a kind of internal flame, bathing its face in a glow like a campfire. It grunted again, guttural.

"The fuck are you after, eh?" The tremor in John's voice betrayed the bravado he tried to show. What was the thing doing here? Sure, they could get territorial around their young, sometimes, but these grass-grazing animals were like upright deer, harmless and pastoral. There was no malice in the creatures, more likely to bolt into a great leaping run than get aggressive. They had been known to grab a dog around the neck, or drown one in a damn if they felt threatened, but they didn't front up to people.

The roo leaned on its front knuckles, pressed its long, thick tail into the bitumen and lifted its back legs, a slow-motion hop forward. John was over six feet tall but he looked up to see the roo's face. The massive red male had to be at least seven foot, towering over him. He'd never seen anything like it. Its balls swung in the night, metronomic. It grunted a third time.

"Fuck's sake." John stood up to his full height, opened his chest up and lifted his arms to either side like he was carrying milk pails. "FUCK OFF, YA CUNT!" he bellowed, sure the animal would decide there was no value in a confrontation.

It leaped forward, covered the six feet between them with ease, and clamped its front paws onto John's shoulders. Black, almost human fingers gripped, each with a two-inch long claw that dug in. The claws all popped through the cotton of his shirt and then his skin with ease. The pain was sudden and electric.

John yelped, whipped one hand up and over, and cracked the roo across the jaw with his heavy fist and not inconsiderable strength. It was a solid blow that would have floored anyone. He grinned. A shame he couldn't have landed one like that on Pat fucken McDonough just now. The roo's head whipped to the side, John's knuckles singing with the satisfyingly solid impact. But the roo slowly turned its head back to face him.

"Tough fucker, eh?" John hauled back to punch again.

The roo leaned back, took all its weight on that fat, meaty tail, and kicked out. Its back foot was longer than John's arm, with three toes. Two small ones to either side, and a central one that was long, strong, and armed with a thick, sharp, black claw, longer than John's hand. That middle claw drove into his gut, pushing all the wind out of the big man as he flew backwards and skidded painfully across the road on his back. His shirt was instantly drenched with blood. Then the agony kicked in, his stomach afire with pain.

"What the fuck is this?" John muttered, staggering to his feet. A slick shifting under his ripped shirt made him gag, fresh pain washing outwards into every nerve. He grabbed at his abdomen, knew his gathered up shirt and his palm had taken the place of the flesh supposed to stop his insides coming out. "To the pub," he said stupidly, thinking only of getting back, getting help.

He stumbled backwards, but the roo leaped, kicking out one huge back leg as it landed. The thick, horny claw slammed into his forehead and ripped downwards as the animal landed, butterflying his face. John howled as flaps of skin opened to either side, blood flooding over his eyes. He hit the bitumen on one shoulder, coughing and gasping for breath. His insides shifted sideways, further than they should ever have been able to. He tried to call for help, but gurgled. The giant roo leaned down, eyes filled with fire. Its mouth opened, revealing long sharp fangs instead of the flat, ruminant molars it should have.

"Isss not right," John slurred through rent lips. "Iss not natural…"

That mouth closed over his neck, furnace hot, its breath a thick, cloying sulphurous cloud. John felt himself dragged along the tarmac, several metres, then the teeth clamped tighter, fresh waves of agony. The flesh of his neck peeled up and away with a wet tear. The roo slapped its mouth, gulped noisily and hissed its pleasure. Darkness swam in to the edges of John's vision. The last thing he felt was its sharp teeth closing over his arm, then the road sliding underneath him again and becoming dirt and dust. Pain overwhelmed him and the darkness swallowed him down.

2

"Come on, Kylie. You know you want to!"

Kylie Timmins shook her head, staring out the side window of the car at endless grass and red dirt, contrasted under starlight. "Nah, Jake. I don't, not really."

Jake's face fell, he pouted, but there was something a little angry in there too. "Come on, don't be a fucken tease!"

"Fuck you, I gave ya a hand job! Be happy with that." She knew she should have told him to go jump when they were in the pub, but he'd promised some good weed if she went with him. That was a worth a quick hand job, but now she wanted to go home. The weed hadn't even been all that strong, mostly leaf. Trust a loser like Jake to buy weed and get no bud.

"I wanna shag, Kylie, come on!"

"No! You bastards gotta learn that no means no. And especially not out here in your battered old Commodore like a couple of teenagers."

Jake barked a laugh. "We are teenagers."

"We're nineteen. Time to mature a bit."

"No one'll see anything. My dad never comes out the back of this paddock, even the bloody cows rarely come here. No one'll disturb us. We could probably camp out here for a week and not see a soul." He reached out his skinny arms, long-fingered hands fumbling around with her breasts, trying to unbutton her shirt.

She slapped his hands away. "Jake, I said no. It's nearly two in the morning, I gotta be at the IGA for work at nine. Take me home."

"Todd Stinson said you bang like a dunny door in a gale. What's he got that I haven't?"

She turned dark eyes to him. "Todd said what?"

Jake pawed at her chest again, whining like a slapped dog.

"Get offa me fucken tits, Jake!"

A thump shook the car slightly.

"What was that?" Kylie twisted in the seat, looking out into the dark, lit only by the blanket of stars.

"What about a blowie, then?" Jake said, voice low and husky. He probably thought it sounded sexy, alluring. His shaggy blond hair fell forward over his eyes.

Kylie ignored him, straightened her flannel shirt as she turned to look out the back window. A shadow lurched past. "Jake! Someone's out there!"

"I told you, no one for fucken miles."

"I saw them, you moron! Someone's there."

Jake sat back, frowning. "Yer a prick tease, you know that?"

Kylie's mouth fell open as a large silhouette leaned close to the driver's side window behind Jake. It was massive, muscular like a bodybuilder, and covered in red fur. Was it a kangaroo? How could it possibly be that big?

"What's the matter?" Jake asked.

She lifted one shaking hand, pointed over his shoulder. The roo leaned closer, pushed its long snout right up to the glass. Its breath huffed, left a cloud of condensation, and its eyes burst into orange flame.

"The fuck!?" Kylie yelped, high-pitched, as the roo's front paws smashed into the car's window. It shattered into a thousand glass cubes that rained all over Jake.

He spun around, forming some angry shout, but those stubby-fingered roo hands with their black claws stretched in and grabbed him either side of the face. Jake squealed, the claws raking deep runnels through his cheeks, then he was being hauled out. His legs kicked, his jeans fly still undone as his hips bounced up over the door and the massive roo pulled him out into the night.

Kylie stared through the broken window, her entire body wracked with shakes. Jake screamed and thrashed in the roo's grasp, but it wasn't letting go. It stretched up to its full height, the biggest, most muscle-bound thing she'd ever seen, and it tipped its head back to roar at the stars. The noise was feral, animalistic, unlike anything she'd ever heard from a kangaroo. It still held either side of Jake's head, lifting the lad up as it stretched. His feet kicked at the ground, stirred up dry grass and orange sand as his fingers scrabbled uselessly at the thing's vice-like grip. The roo's lips peeled back, revealing long, sharpened teeth glistening with spit. Kylie shook her head. *Roos don't have teeth like that*, she thought stupidly, staring at one that absolutely, clearly did.

The roo roared again and flexed its huge shoulders. Its chest muscles pumped up, bunched like half soccer balls. Jake's screams increased a full octave. He pummelled at the black paws digging into the sides of his head, his eyes wide. The whites were bright in the night, then the roo pumped its muscles again and Jake's head burst like a ripe fruit. Kylie screamed as blood and brains and shards of skull sprayed out, some of it spattering onto the dashboard and steering wheel through the shattered window. A bloody length of blond hair lay over the wing mirror.

Piss soaked her jean shorts, but she ignored it,

scrambled over into the driver's seat, clawing for the keys in the ignition. She found them as the roo dropped Jake's limp body and turned back to look at her. Its eyes blazed with fire. Gore dripped from its fur. It grunted through sharp teeth.

Kylie turned the keys and the old Commodore coughed and something metal grinded against itself, but it roared into life, a cloud of exhaust billowing out behind. She thumped into the driver's seat, rammed the car into gear, and floored the accelerator. Wheels spun, dirt and grass flew up in a curving rooster tail as she cranked the wheel to turn the car in a hard U-turn. She half-circled the roo, driving a donut Jake would have enjoyed, and aimed straight for the gate out of the paddock and the dirt road beyond. Running entirely on instinct, she hit the rough track and leaned over the wheel, the car gaining speed. Thirty kilometres per hour. Forty, fifty, sixty. It shook and rattled, shimmied left and right on the rough, corrugated road.

She chanced a look in the mirror and screamed again as the massive roo covered some thirty feet in a single bound and came down on the boot of the car with a deafening crunch of metal. The back end sunk, the front of the car lurching up into the air and Kylie briefly saw a wide expanse of stars before the Commodore swerved crazily and started collecting fence wire, slewing out of control.

"No, no, no!" she cried, tears of shock and fear clouding her vision.

The roof dented in with a boom like a giant drum. Then again, and those black, sharp-clawed paws punched through. The car went sideways, a fencepost slammed into the driver's door, bending it in far enough to crack Kylie's elbow. The back wheels hit a rain channel and the car bounced, turned a half circle and skidded backwards. She tried to rev it, but the engine wailed, the car somehow out of gear. As she tried to find the clutch, ram the gear stick across, the roof peeled back like tin foil. Kylie screamed again as the massive roo leaned in, its mouth opening wide. She saw those teeth, its flame-orange eyes, smelled something like rotten eggs and smoke, and then the burning hot mouth slammed into her face and she saw nothing more.

3

"**Your wife come** back yet?" Shane Keene asked.

Bill Catter turned from looking at rolls of barbed wire, hands stuffed into the pockets of his ubiquitous tan Hard Yakka work shorts. "Nah. Did yours?"

Shane was taken aback. "Fair fucken go, Bill. You don't come back from dying of breast cancer, ya cunt." Truth told, even after three years he wasn't used to it. The two of them had run the country store in town for nearly forty years before she died, and Shane kept telling himself he'd retire. It was harder than ever without her, and he was old enough to call it quits. Sell up and move somewhere near the sea maybe. As if any dumb bastard would buy this business.

Bill sniffed, shrugged. "Yeah, well mine ain't come back either."

Shane dragged a hand over his long, grey beard. "You are one onerous cunt, Bill Catter. No one in town is surprised she fucked off, you know. Amazing it didn't happen sooner."

Bill turned back again, face thunderous, then let out a bellow of laugh. "Fuck ya. It's only been three days. She'll be back."

"Four, isn't it?"

Bill frowned. "Yeah, maybe four. Whatever." He dumped a heavy coil of barbed wire on the counter and dug around in his shorts for a wallet. "You seen the blood out front?"

"Out front of my shop?"

"Nah, next door. In front of Carol's Café."

"How much blood?"

Catter handed over cash, took his change. "A fuckload. Someone must have flattened a roo or a wombat or something in the night."

Keene frowned. "Out on the highway, maybe, but not right in town here. Not going fast enough, surely."

Catter shrugged. "Maybe. No carcass either, but what else would it be?"

Keene pursed his lips, nodded, and muttered, "Yeah nah" because he had no better theory.

He watched Catter's broad back as the man walked out, bow-legged and belligerent. Since his wife had died, Keene missed out on a lot of town gossip. A fella needed a line into the Country Women's Association to really know what went on around here, but it didn't take James Bond to work out that Bill treated Pauline Catter badly. It wasn't unusual in the country to hear about domestic violence. It was almost expected. Hard people working hard land, seemingly constant drought, never enough subsidies, the isolation. But it didn't have to be like that. Shane and his dear departed had barely shared a cross word. He liked to think most of the fellas in town were decent sorts, even if they were rough and ready. They weren't violent, especially to women. Sure, they punched on with each other often enough, but that was normal men's business, like Pat and John last night. He smiled. Pat had given John what for in that encounter, John was lucky Kealan threw him out, save him any more embarrassment. For a small bloke, Pat was a tenacious opponent. He reminded Shane of a staffy and that only made him sad again. His dog had been dead two years now as well. Maybe it was time for a new pup, stop him being such a melancholy prick.

But Shane didn't like the idea of that men-in-the-pub attitude carrying over into the home, being meted out to the wife and kids. Yet it wasn't rare, and Bill Catter was a poster boy for it. His kids had both fucked off first chance they got, his daughter had had haunted eyes since she was eight or ten. His son always showed the bruises of Catter's lessons. Still teens when they left, the both of them, Pauline left alone with Bill, though no doubt pleased the kids had got away at least.

Pauline had nowhere to go, according to Shane's wife, and no money to start over. A common enough story. She said there were plenty of women in town who wouldn't be in town if they could afford to leave. Keene sighed. Tough life in every way.

He wandered out the front of his shop, squinting against the incandescent sun, the hot, dry breeze. Sure enough, there on the tarmac outside Carol's Café was a patch of blood like you'd expect from a roo that went under a truck wheel. Maybe a truck had come through late. The blood smeared off the side the of the road and past the end of the café. Shane frowned, followed it. It went a few metres, then stopped, a few drops around the area and then he lost the trail. He was no tracker. Maybe he should ask Colin Mawber.

He checked himself. Was it racist to assume a blackfella was a tracker? Mawber was a cow hand for Pat McDonough, so he shouldn't make any more assumptions than that. Perhaps whatever had been hit had dragged itself this far, then died. So where was the carcass?

"Bit fucken grim, ey?"

Keene turned, saw Tracy Robinson standing on the pavement outside Carol's. Carol herself stood beside Robinson. *Two ends of the spectrum there*, Keene thought to himself. Tracy Robinson was young, slim, shapely, shoulder length dark hair framing a heart-shaped pretty face. Carol Monroe was a widow, seventy if she was a day, her hair a wispy cloud of dyed purple over a face with more wrinkles than Shane's ballsack. Her back was bent and her knees swollen. But she'd been a looker in her day, Shane remembered. She was only about a decade older than him, after all. And he wasn't exactly the robust youth he'd been. He rested a hand on the rotund belly stretching his cotton shirt, then quickly moved it away, self-conscious.

Both women were looking at the blood in the road.

"Something met a sticky end," Carol said, and laughed ruefully. "Coffee, Shane?"

"Sure, thanks. And a bacon and egg roll? I'm so hungry I could eat a horse and chase the jockey."

"I'll bring it around to you next door."

"Thanks, Carol, yer blood's worth bottling."

Tracy had a takeaway cup in hand. "I'd better get to work."

"Time to open up already?" Keene asked her. "Can't be ten o'clock yet!"

She grimaced, shook her head. "Got some fixing up to do. John Lynch and Pat McDonough had a set-to last night, busted a couple of chairs. Said I'd fix them before we opened today." She frowned. "Wait, you were there. You saw 'em, couple of fuckwits they are."

"Yeah, I saw." Shane grinned. Tracy smiled crookedly shook her head. "You behind the bar after that?" he asked.

Tracy let out a humourless bark of a laugh. "Where the fuck else would I be? I'll grow old and die behind that bar."

"There are worse places to be," Carol Monroe said. "But not many. Pretty young girl, you should get out while you can. Head to the city, don't stay here where everything's getting old."

Tracy smiled. "I'm saving up, don't you worry."

"I'll see you for a couple of lunchtime schooners in a few hours then," Shane said, and gave them both a smile before heading back into the country store. He missed his wife more than ever.

4

Pat McDonough wandered into the IGA supermarket in the main street to find something for his lunch. He planned to get most of his lunch from the George Hotel like most days, but he needed something solid first. The IGA usually had a few bread rolls or pastries that would do the trick. Maybe a pie or a sausage roll. When he was really hungry he went to Carol's, but Sheila had made him a big breakfast earlier, and that would last. But he was tired. It had been a hard morning's yakka already, the day hot as hell, and his help nowhere to be seen.

"G'day, Pat."

He turned, saw Rich Duncan in the line for the checkout holding a large bag of potato chips. "How ya goin', Rich?"

"I could complain, but what's the fucken point, ey?"

"Hear that."

Rich tipped his head to one side. "You okay, mate? You look ragged."

"Long day already. Fucken Jake never showed up this morning, had to shift all the feed bales meself."

"Jake?"

"Long streak of piss, young bloke helps me out. Got that shaggy blond hair."

Rich laughed. "I remember. You're not wrong about skinny. Probably has to run around in the shower to get wet."

"That's him."

"Never showed up today, ey? Was he in the George

last night?"

"At first, yeah, but he left early. A hangover I could understand. But just not there, that's weird, even for him. For all his mooning about, he's a conscientious kid really. Good help, too, strong for all his lack of meat." Pat shrugged. "I'm sure he'll show up."

Sally, standing patiently behind the checkout, raised an eyebrow. "Hey, doesn't Jake run with that young tart Kylie Small?"

Pat nodded. "Yeah, I've seen 'em together, canoodling. In fact, they might have left the pub together last night."

Sally sniffed, turned her lip. "She never showed up here to work this morning either."

Rich Duncan clicked his tongue like he was calling a horse. "There it is then. Probably still tangled in the sheets together somewhere, horny little buggers."

"You're just jealous," Sally said with a laugh.

"That I am! My wife hasn't tangled me in sheets since the last time it rained."

"Fuck me," Pat laughed. "That is a long time."

Rich made a pained expression, but then grinned. He paid for his chips and Pat grabbed a sausage roll from the heated cabinet beside the till and gave Sally a five dollar note.

"Schooner?" he asked.

Rich pursed his lips. "Supposed to be shifting my stock to the south paddock this arvo, they've eaten themselves to the dirt where they are. It'll be liver flukes next if I'm not careful."

"All the more reason to wet your whistle first."

"You've convinced me."

The George was still inside, cool from the night before but warming up. Dusts motes drifted in sunlight lancing through the windows. A long bar on the far wall had a forest of beer pumps, ice-covered under their garish labels. Above the bar were dented hubcaps and pictures of women with painted on clothes and nothing else. Around the walls hung drawings and etchings of Morgan Creek's early days, when the main street was dirt. Most of the buildings looked the same, just with more space between them, modern shops slowly filling the gaps over the years. A line of silver barstools with red plastic tops stood at the bar and several polished wood tables and chairs were scattered throughout the open bar space, occupied by a handful of townsfolk. The place smelled of beer and hot chips from the bistro, which Pat always thought was a fancy word to describe the small kitchen that fried frozen fish fillets or chicken schnitzels and little else. Then again, Kealan or Tracy could put together a half decent burger in there.

"Mornin', gents," Kealan Burke said from behind the bar. "Two?"

"Thank you, Kealan," Pat said. "Mornin', Tracy."

"How are you today?"

"All the better for seeing you."

Tracy frowned. "I'd be charmed if I knew you didn't see every woman the same way."

"They are all the same. I can't cuddle any of 'em."

"Away with ya." She turned and went down the trap door behind the bar into the cellar.

Bill Catter sat on a high stool at the end of the bar nursing a schooner, scowling like always. Pat pursed his lips. "Bill," he said perfunctorily.

"Pat."

"Bill," said Rich.

"Rich."

Charles Rutledge, the town's divorced mechanic, sat at a table alone under the window, a schooner of his own half drunk. "Pat. Rich," he said.

"Charlie," they both replied.

"Jesus fucked a stump," Tracy said, unable to suppress a laugh as she appeared back behind the bar. "The depth of philosophical debate in this pub never ceases to amaze me."

The men all grinned despite themselves, even Bill Catter's lip half-quirked. Then they fell into silence again, drinking.

Eventually Pat asked of no one in particular, "John Lynch been in today?"

A variety of sounds in the negative and shaking heads. Several grins and nods too. Word got around, even among those who hadn't been there.

"You whipped him last night," Kealan said. "Probably home licking his wounds."

"He gave as good as he got," Pat said, tongue running over the torn skin inside his lower lip. It was still sore.

"Nah," Charlie Rutledge said. "He got the worst of that and he knows it."

"He shouldn't mouth off then, ey."

"Quite right. He'll be back tonight, I expect."

"You blokes seen that blood in the road outside Carol's," Bill Catter said.

Conversation fell to theories of what kind of animal and what kind of vehicle had combined to make the mess and they all knew they were shooting shit with no real purpose. The closest thing to camaraderie between the hard-bitten country men.

Sheila McDonough came in through the pub doors, surprising Pat. His wife rarely entered what she called the den of thieves. That made no sense to Pat, but his wife was often given to unexplainable turns of phrase. The others there launched into whoops of caution and comments like "Look out, Pat!" and "Here comes trouble!" Sheila withstood it for a few moments, eyes hard, and the men fell awkwardly silent. Pat smiled to himself. The leader of this town's Country Women's Association brooked no shit from anyone.

"You all finished?" she asked. "Bunch of bloody schoolboys."

Kealan guffawed, leaning on a Tooheys New pump crusted with ice. "What can I get ya, Sheila?"

"Nothin'. I knew my good for nothing old man would be here. Pat, where's Jake?"

"No idea. I was just telling Rich earlier that he never showed up this morning."

Sheila's eyebrows cinched together. "His mother is worried sick. He never came home last night."

"Try Kylie's place," Charlie said. "Those two are bumpin' uglies, aren't they?"

"On and off," Sheila said with a nod. "But I'm not new here, Charlie, I checked there first."

The pub sank into silence. Then Pat said, "Was anyone there? At Kylie's?"

"Only her father, and he's not really a fount of information."

Pat nodded. Jack Small was a deadbeat alcoholic, the kind who stayed home and drank rather than socialise at the George. Kylie often had bruises, and Pat suspected Jack had delivered them. The man probably didn't give a shit where his daughter was, and his wife had left years ago. Kylie would be up and gone before long, he suspected. It was a mild surprise she hadn't already left. Maybe there was some vestige of loyalty to her father still in her somewhere. Love was a complicated thing.

"I was in the IGA earlier," he said. "Kylie didn't show up for work either, Sally said."

"Probably fucken eloped together," Bill Catter said.

Sheila gave him a hard stare. "If any of you blokes see either of 'em, you tell 'em to get home and let their parents know they're safe," she said.

She left the pub to murmurings of consent.

Pat sipped at his beer, an uneasy feeling he couldn't quite explain squirming in his gut.

5

Stu Stred hated the job, but he couldn't do anything else. Driving from one pisspot outback town to another, all the surly, parochial farmers he had to deal with. It made him miserable. But at least he wasn't one of them, he often reflected. Rather spend his life selling them fertilizer and feed than be some loser scratching in the dirt for living. That was no life. Not so long ago he'd arrived at a farm for an arranged visit to find no one home, or so he thought. He'd walked around the house to see if anyone was out the back and had found the poor bastard swinging from a nylon rope off the back veranda, feet circling a metre off the ground, the man's head swollen, purple, and fly blown. The land out here had a way of breaking people.

It had taken Stred two hours to drive over to Morgan Creek from Patterson and he was bracing himself for another set of forced smiles, another round of convincing these bastards his company was better than the competition. He wished he could do it all over the phone from his office, but face to face was the country way, he'd learned that long ago. No one out here trusted city folk, you had to come and show yourself.

He checked his list and saw John Lynch at the top, the big muscly farmer who ran a property not far from town. The other farms he planned to visit were on the far side, so he'd do those after lunch. A steak sandwich from Carol's Café and then a few schooners in the George Hotel on the way through would do it. Morgan Creek wasn't all bad.

He blew out a breath and turned off the single lane highway, up the narrow road that led to Lynch's driveway. Another few kilometres and he was bouncing along the dirt track leading to the farmhouse. Their appointment was for 1pm and it was a quarter to, so he might have to wait. Country time often meant an hour late. It rarely meant any time early. He'd stay in the air-conditioned comfort of his car in that case, read a book. He had the latest Lee Child on the back seat to enjoy during any stops and in the motel later.

He pulled up to the farmhouse gate, wincing at the pressure of heat and dryness as he hopped out to open it up. He drove over the cattle grid, making his tyres rattle, then got out to close the gate again. He sat for a moment enjoying the AC, then drove on up the hill to the house.

As he pulled up, he noticed Lynch's ute wasn't anywhere in sight. Better knock anyway, he thought, just in case. Then go back to his car and wait. He stepped out of his comfort and said, "Oof" as the heat of the day punched him in the face again. It was even hotter up here than down by the gate, if that was possible. Dry and dusty, smelling of grass and drought and cow shit. He grimaced and walked up to the ratty old weatherboard house. The paint peeled from the woodwork, the tin roof rusty and crooked. Lynch lived alone here, Stred knew that. Another one whose wife had left him, whose children had grown up and gone to the city. The legacy of farming families was dying out like the drought-stricken grass in country Australia. Big farming conglomerates were taking over, or the industry was simply drying up like an outback creek bed. He wondered how long his job might last. Might need to look into selling something else.

Sure enough, no one answered the door.

Stred turned back to his car, looking forward to the AC again, and jumped. "Fuck me," he muttered.

The biggest roo he'd ever seen stood by the almost-new silver Toyota Camry. It had to be seven feet tall, so muscular it seemed almost a parody. He'd seen big, muscly reds before, but nothing like this bastard. They stared at each other for a moment.

"Hungry or something?" Stred said. The place was dry as a dead dingo's dick, but there was scrubby yellow grass everywhere, and these animals were designed to subsist on that, weren't they?

The roo leaned forward, put its front knuckles to the dirt and swung its massive back legs through, taking one big roo step closer to him. Then it stood up tall again. Stred frowned. Fear wormed into his gut. There were stories about roos being territorial, but they weren't aggressive. At least, he thought they weren't. Yet this one seemed to emanate malice. He backed up onto John Lynch's porch.

The roo leaned forward and took another swinging step closer.

"You are one big fucken unit, aren't ya," Stred said, his voice tremulous. "Fuck off, ey?" He tried to look around for something to throw at the thing while simultaneously not taking his eyes off it.

The roo opened its mouth and made a kind of hissing, grunting noise. The mouth continued to open, far too wide, unnaturally so, and was forested with sharp teeth.

"The fuck...?" Stred looked properly left and right and realised he'd trapped himself by backing into the small enclosed porch.

The roo took another step forward. Stred patted his pockets, looking for anything he could use as a weapon. He found a ballpoint pen in his shirt pocket and pointed it at the roo like a knife. "You fuck off, ya big bastard. Hear me? Fuck off!" The pen shook in his grip and he felt at least as stupid as he thought he must look.

Still on the dirt at the bottom of the three steps leading up to the porch, the roo stretched up, leaned forward. It came eye level with Stred as his back bumped into the front door. Country folk, his mind said. They leave everything unlocked. His hand fumbled behind him, found the doorknob and twisted it. The door opened and he fell inside.

"Oh, thank fuck!"

He turned and started to run, aiming for anywhere away from that monstrous beast outside, but his stiff white collar pulled suddenly tight and jerked him back. He coughed and gagged as it bit into his throat. The roo's sharp claws raked the back of his neck, its other front paw coming around to grip his face. He smelled the musky, dusty odour of its fur, and something else. Something spicy, smoky.

Stred stabbed furiously backwards with the pen, felt it banging into the roo's thick hide, skidding left and right. Then there was a plastic crack and it snapped in two. "Fucking hell," Stred wailed as the roo dragged him backwards.

It put one paw under his chin and tipped his head back. He stared up into its rough, furred face as it stared down at him with orange eyes that seemed to be made of fire. He even felt the heat from them. It slipped one thickly muscled arm under his chin and Stred struggled and blubbered but was held fast. It wrapped its other arm around his chest, hugging him against its hard, bulging body. Slowly, staring with those fiery eyes, it bunched up its strength and pulled his head upwards. Stred's mouth was clenched shut by the furry elbow under his chin and he snorted with pain and a desperate need for breath. He kicked and thrashed, realised his feet were swinging free as it lifted him easily off the ground. Its elbow levered up and up, its other arm like a steel clamp across his chest. The beast's breath was hotter than a desert wind, but it breathed easily, expending no real effort at all as Stred's neck made sickening, sharp popping sounds accompanied by more pain than he'd ever known. He screamed in agony through his clenched teeth and blacked out in the same moment the roo tore his head clean off his neck.

6

The Country Women's Association hall on the edge of town was a little dilapidated on the outside, but spick and span inside. Sheila McDonough prided herself on its internal neatness, and reminded herself again to hassle Pat about getting some of the men together to paint the exterior. The CWA could afford the paint, but that kind of labour was the sort of thing that would keep the blokes out of trouble for a while. Let them work as hard as the women every now and then.

Sharon Duncan, Rich's wife, pulled up in her husband's old ute as Sheila unlocked the door. She waited for the woman to join her, enjoying the slightly cooler evening air.

"How are you, dear?" Sheila asked.

"Sore and a little annoyed, if I'm honest."

"Oh?"

"Spent the day trying to get three people's work done all on my own."

Sheila frowned, something uncomfortable taking up residence in her gut. "What do you mean?"

"Well," Sharon shook her head. "I know it's a small town, but when those two agreed to split rents with me and we combined the newsagency with their haberdashery, it was agreed we wouldn't make life difficult for each other."

"You're talking about Greta and Brigitte?" Sharon ran the town newsagency, mostly selling newspapers, cigarettes and Lotto tickets, while Rich took care of the farm, with help from other Morgan Creek locals, and occasional blow-ins. It had been that way for as long as

Sheila could remember. But a town this small had slow trade in all things, so when Greta and Brigitte arrived, looking for a place to sell clothes and offer seamstress repairs, the combination of their work seemed a good fit. Sharon had too much room in the newsagency and splitting the rent solved a lot of problems. Greta and Brigitte didn't need much space, and all three women got on well.

Sheila smiled. Even if the two haberdashers did live and work together while the town did its best not to notice. Sheila thought they were lovely women who deserved each other and she believed they were quite happy together. And good for them.

"Of course Greta and Brigitte," Sharon said. "They didn't show up today and there were several customers all expecting to pick up repairs. I'm a little annoyed they didn't even phone."

"You rang them?"

"Certainly, but they didn't answer."

Sheila pursed her lips, thinking back to the pub earlier. Jake and Kylie both not showing up for work today. Now Brigitte and Greta. Their house was a small cottage right on the southern outskirts of Morgan Creek, subdivided off when old man Morton had decided to divest himself of some land in retirement. Something seemed off about it all. She glanced down the road toward the George Hotel. Pat would be back in there necking schooners by now, maybe she should talk to him. Another car pulled up. After the meeting, she decided. She'd drop into the pub and see if anyone else had seen or heard from Greta or Brigitte. Or if anyone else had been reported missing.

"Hey, look out, Pat! She's here to drag you home!"

Sheila scowled. "Again, really? Do put a sock in it, Charles Rutledge!"

The rest of the patrons whooped in joy as Charlie laughed and raised his glass in an acquiescent toast.

"Everything all right?" Pat asked, eyebrows cinched together.

"I don't know. Buy me a drink."

"Gin and tonic, please, Tracy," Pat said, and the young girl behind the bar nodded.

"Did Jake show up this afternoon?"

Pat shook his head. "Nope."

"Greta and Brigitte didn't go to work either."

Pat narrowed his eyes, and Sheila saw her own concerns mirrored there. "What's up with everyone in town lately?" he asked.

"Exactly what I'm wondering."

Pat rubbed at his chin, looked around the pub. He'd told Sheila about the dust up with John Lynch, and she realised he was subconsciously touching the bruise the man had left him.

"Kealan," Pat called out.

"Another one, mate?"

"Oh, yeah. All right, thanks. But I was going to ask if you saw John today at all."

"Nah, not yet."

"He's normally here by now."

"Still embarrassed you knocked him on his arse," Kealan said, putting a condensing schooner on the bar. "And probably shitty with me cos I threw him out."

"Yeah, but he always comes back."

"His ute is parked on the verge just outside town like normal," Charlie Rutledge said. "I passed it earlier."

"He always parks up so he can drive home," Rich said, coming out of the Gents and quickly catching up. "He not here?"

Someone else across the bar called over. "The old Mazda ute?"

"That's it," Pat said.

"Been there all day."

Pat, Rich and Charlie exchanged a meaningful look. They all looked at Kealan, leaning palms down, straight-armed on the bar. He lifted his hands and shrugged. Sheila watched them mull it over. Shane Keene sat on a barstool not far away, sipping his beer.

"Normally here by now," he muttered.

"Passing strange," Pat said eventually.

Sheila let out an exasperated breath. "Go and check on your bloody friend, will ya!"

The men looked surprised, but all nodded rapidly. "Yeah. Nah yeah, o'course. Yeah, s'pose we should," Pat said.

"It's late now, though," Charlie said. "It's after ten."

"I'll drive over first thing in the morning," Pat said. "Make sure he's okay. It wouldn't hurt for me to offer an olive branch anyway, John's not a bad bloke."

"Good idea," Shane said.

Kealan Burke said, "I'll come with you, Pat. As I was the one threw him out. Town's too small for grudges. Pick me up?"

"Sure, about eight?"

"Sounds good."

Pat looked at his wife, popped one eyebrow. Why was he checking their plans with her? But she nodded anyway. Something told her the whole thing was a little more urgent, but country life moved at a measured pace. It was unseemly to act rashly. Surely everything would have a simple explanation. The man probably was embarrassed, he was half again Pat's size. Then again, he should know better than to mess with her

Patrick. She was proud, despite her annoyance at these middle-aged fools who should know better than to spend their time fighting each other.

"Be sure you do," she said.

But what about the girls? Brigitte and Greta. And Jake and Kylie? She sighed. Something weird was happening in Morgan Creek. "Get us another G&T, Pat. Now I'm here I might as well make the most of it."

7

Pat McDonough drove along the main street a little after eight the next morning, feeling somewhat dusty from the night before. He had enjoyed maybe a few too many beers. It was a rare pleasure to share his pub time with Sheila and they'd made the most of it. He had a lot of work to do on the farm and had put in a couple of hours already, but still his head ached. He'd have to get back to work as soon as he could, everything harder with the seemingly eternal drought. And still no Jake. Sheila was distributing feed for their stock in the meantime, using the tractor to spread bales of hay in long lines across each paddock. He felt bad leaving her to it, but she was right, they ought to check on John Lynch. Pat allowed himself a smile. It would be good to be the bigger man and, while offering an olive branch, enjoy the other man's discomfort at the beating he took.

He waved to Rose Taylor as she opened up the Rose Boutique, a store that seemed to sell pretty much everything. He couldn't remember a time Sheila's Christmas and birthday presents hadn't come from there. Kealan Burke was leaning against the closed front door of his pub, smoking a rollie while he waited. Tall and dark-haired, slim in worn jeans and t-shirt for some band or other, Kealan had something of a movie star look about him, Pat always thought. He noticed Helen Burke's car parked out front, Kealan's pretty wife obviously returned from visiting her sister in Broken Hill. Pat slowed, leaned out the open window. "Coffee first?" He gestured down the street towards

Carol's Café.

"Excellent idea."

"Helen's back?"

Kealan nodded. "Late last night." He pushed off the door and strolled along the wide footpath while Pat drove on and pulled into a 45-degree angled parking bay right outside Carol's. As he got out Bill Catter pulled in a couple of spaces further up.

"Bill."

"Pat."

"Bill."

"Kealan."

The three of them went inside. The place smelled of hot grease and lavender air freshener. Carol stood behind a counter at the end, a small kitchen behind her. A glass cabinet to one side held pre-made sandwiches, cakes and pastries. A hot cabinet on top had a variety of pies and sausage rolls. Aluminium tables and chairs were neatly organised in two lines down each side of the small café space, pictures on the walls above of drovers and sheep in dusty paddocks, all shot to look exotic and exciting.

"Mornin', gents. Coffees all round?"

They murmured the affirmative and their thanks and stood awkwardly. She knew their various preferences by heart. Eventually Bill Catter said. "Early for you, ain't it, Pat?"

"Going to check on John Lynch, remember? With Kealan here."

"Round two, ey?"

"Nah, just making sure he's all right."

Bill sniffed, nodded. "S'pect he is."

"Yeah."

"Saw his ute still on the side though." Bill gestured back over his shoulder. "Which is a bit weird."

"Exactly," Pat said. "Hence me and Kealan going to check. No harm in looking out for each other, you know."

"Sounds like something a woman would say," Bill said with a bark of a laugh, like he thought that was the worst thing possible.

Pat frowned. "It is what a woman would say. It's what Sheila said. You were there. And you know what, Bill? She's right. It's fucken tough out here, no point in making it tougher by trying to be some kind of macho man."

Bill barked his humourless laugh again. "Whatever ya reckon, mate." He took his coffee from Carol, dropped a five dollar note in her hand, then pointed to the tin on her counter that said *Help farmers in need* on it. "Change in there."

His neighbour had shot himself in the face with a shotgun the year before and Bill seemed to have been deeply affected by it, though he would never admit as much. But Pat had noticed he always put his change in that tin, and Bill wasn't the kind to have much change to spare. There's nothing more complicated than folk, he thought wryly.

"Thanks, Bill." Carol dropped the coins in.

Bill grinned at Pat and Kealan. "Tell John Lynch I've still got an old change table at home somewhere if it'll make it easier for you lot with his nappies."

Pat sighed.

Without waiting for a reply, Bill headed out. Carol handed over coffees to Pat and Kealan. "He's an abrasive arsehole," she said. "But it's all front."

"Clear from his change going in there every day," Kealan said, pointing to the farmer's fund tin on her counter. So he'd noticed too.

"Exactly."

There was a moment of quiet, then Carol said, "Reach out to him as well, ey? Both of ya are good blokes, you can make the first move. It must be hard since Pauline left him, he must be lonely."

"Deserves to be lonely really," Pat said, staring out the big window at the front of the café.

"I know, we've all heard the rumours. I'm glad Pauline got out. But Bill is a troubled man. See if you can't show him some kindness. It goes a long way. He might change."

"Now that does sound like something a woman would say," Kealan said. "Sheila especially."

Pat laughed. "Sheila did say exactly that when word got out that Pauline had gone."

"And I say it too." Carol patted their shoulders, one hand on each. "Think about it, lads, ey?"

"We will. You're right, of course."

"Carol's always right." Shane Keene gave them all a big grin as he came in, twenty-year old Blundstone boots clomping on the tiled floor. "But what about this time?"

"That we should try to show Bill Catter some kindness," Pat said.

Shane's eyebrows shot up. "Yeah nah, he can stick it up his arse. That shitcunt doesn't have a kind bone in his body, I'm not wasting mine on him."

There was a moment of silence. Pat knew all the men there agreed with Shane. A man could only be a dick for so long before everyone gave up on him. But Carol's eyes were sad. It was possible, he supposed, for them all to be right.

"Coffee, love?" Carol said to Shane.

"Yes, please. And a bacon and egg roll? I'm so hungry I could eat the arse out of a low flying duck."

"Coming right up."

"We'd best be off," Pat said. "Come on, Kealan."

They drank their coffee as Pat drove them out of town, and past John Lynch's ute parked up on the roadside only a couple of hundred metres after Carol's. Pat slowed and they both leaned over to look. It was nothing they didn't expect, dirty with red dust, papers and takeaway coffee cups on the dash and passenger seat. A tarp and a few random tools in the tray. Pat sped up again and they arrived at Lynch's farm only a few minutes later. Kealan climbed out, opened the gate to let Pat through, closed it behind him.

"Got a weird feeling about this," Kealan said as he got back into Pat's ute.

Pat nodded, grateful it wasn't just him. "Sheila was talking at home last night about how lots of people seem to be AWOL lately. She was full of G&Ts and in a strop, but I've felt uncomfortable since. Didn't sleep well."

"Me either."

As they drove up the long dirt driveway, slowly uphill towards Lynch's tatty farmhouse, silence fell again. They saw the back end of a silver Camry parked a little way back from the house.

"Oh, maybe he has visitors," Kealan said. "That would explain him not being around much."

Pat pursed his lips as he slowed to a stop behind the Toyota. "I recognise that car for some reason." He killed the engine.

They got out and Kealan said, "Jesus fuck and fucken Mary!" a moment before Pat saw what shocked the publican.

A body lay in the driveway, at the foot of the porch steps. It wore grey slacks, a white collared shirt, but no tie, and shiny black shoes. But it had no head. The red dust was almost black in a fan from the ragged neck, where blood had flooded. Pat swallowed down bile as they both ran over to it. Flies swarmed up from the corpse and clouded around as they stared.

"Where the fuck is his fucken head?" Kealan demanded.

Pat looked up, saw the farmhouse door standing open. "John?" he yelled. "John Lynch, you here?" Had the lunatic blown someone's head off with his shotgun?

He exchanged a glance with Kealan and they moved forward together, cautiously side by side up the steps. It didn't take too long to walk through all the rooms of the house and find them empty. Lynch's bachelor lifestyle was evident everywhere, even down to the skin mags on the coffee table in the lounge room. Dirty dishes were stacked in the kitchen sink, another haven for flies. The bathroom smelled of coal tar soap, the basin peppered with beard shavings.

Pat sucked in a deep breath, then let it slowly out. Shook his head. "What the fuck?"

"He's not here, but his ute is where he left it the other night."

"Yep, which leaves us with two questions. Where the fuck is he and who the fuck is that poor headless cunt out there?"

Kealan nodded, licked his lips. "Good questions both."

Pat frowned, looked back towards the front of the house. "I'm sure I've seen that Camry before."

"We should call the cops," Kealan said.

"We should, but Gomzi will be ages getting here. Come on." Pat went back out the front, held his breath and crouched beside the headless corpse. He suppressed a gag at the stiff feel of the body as he rifled its pockets. He found a wallet, stepped back with it as the flies descended again on the spilled blood and torn flesh. It didn't look anything like a shotgun blast to him. The skin of the neck seemed torn, a stub of bone sticking out.

He opened the wallet, found a driver's licence, and nodded in understanding. "Of course. This is Stu Stred."

"You know him?"

"All the famers around here do. He's a salesman, always trying to get us to upgrade our balers and tractors and shit, buy more fertilizer. Comes around every few months trying to butter us up."

"You think he came around here and John Lynch killed him?" Kealan asked. "And that's why John's fucked off? He's on the run?"

Pat shook his head. "Look at that state of the poor cunt's neck. Look at the fucken bone sticking out. Something tore that head off, Kealan. John's big, and toey as a Roman sandal, but no one is that strong, are they?"

"Machine accident?"

"You see any machines around?"

"Fucken hell."

"Fucken hell."

They stood staring. Pat's stomach roiled like he'd eaten something bad. His brain skidded around trying to come up with an explanation for the state of the body in the dirt at his feet, but nothing would stick.

He turned and headed back for his ute. "Let's get back. You call Steve Gomzi on the way and we'll see who else is there."

"And do what?"

"I don't fucken know, Kealan, but this situation is too much for us to handle alone. People die out here all the time, sure, but not like that!"

"Fair point."

8

Scott Moses cursed his old bones as he sank into the armchair under the ceiling fan. He cursed the heat, the endless drought, the ravages of age that had taken his wife a few years before. He clicked on the television and settled back with a cold lemonade to watch the quiz shows he enjoyed. Life as a widower was no fun, but he didn't have it too bad. His daughter would be along in a few days, with her husband and kids, all coming to stay for a week. Genuinely something to look forward to, and he knew a lot of folk didn't have that. He smiled. His bones ached, but life wasn't so bad. He wished Marsha was still here to share it with him, but otherwise he couldn't really complain.

A scream pierced the hot midday stillness.

Scott dug around for the remote he'd just dropped and pressed the button to send the volume back down. Had that really been a scream? It sounded so–

Another scream, high and bloodcurdling. Scott frowned, hauled himself up from his chair. His acre was the last but one on the edge of the town proper. One more property, the LaFaro's place, stood after his before the road stretched out into farmland. Morgan Creek had a single main street with virtually all the commerce on it, a few side streets with some industry, like Charlie Rutledge's workshop, then houses scattered in a rough grid that petered out into farmland in every direction after a few hundred metres. A human blemish on the pristine outback, Marsha had called Morgan Creek, but they loved it here. Isolation and country life didn't suit everyone, but it was great for them. For those it didn't suit, however, it could cause problems. Especially if those people desperately wanted to be somewhere else but couldn't move, usually for financial reasons. The LaFaros were like that. Scott knew Brennan wanted to move his family to a bigger town, even somewhere like Broken Hill. Still remote, but not nearly so small and isolated. But they couldn't afford it. And that caused tension. He heard Brennan and Cindy arguing sometimes. He heard them yelling at their teenage kids, and heard Carl and Natasha yelling back. It must be hard. But Scott was also fairly convinced Brennan had never fallen to violence. He didn't drink heavily like so many others around here did. But those screams. Had he finally snapped?

Another scream pierced the hot day.

Scott moved to the window and looked out towards the LaFaro's place about a hundred yards away. He couldn't see much past his double garage and the scrubby blue gums lining their back yard. He frowned, shook his head. It was good to be neighbourly, but one couldn't interfere.

Another scream, loud, angry yelling. And then a gunshot.

Scott jumped, his heart racing, and he hurried to the back door, grabbing his stained and tatty Akubra as he went. News items of family murders, broken fathers committing atrocious murder-suicides of their wife and kids, rattled through his mind.

He was such a nice bloke.
He did so much for the community.
I had no idea they were in so much strife.
Why didn't he ask for help?

"Bloody hell," Scott muttered as he hurried across his back yard. What might he be running into? "Eighty-bloody-four years fucken old, I'm an idiot to be running anywhere."

He climbed over his three-bar fence, carefully stepping down on the LaFaro's side behind their garage. He hurried around it and skidded to a stop, mouth falling open. His dentures shifted in his suddenly slack jaw and he shoved them back with his tongue. They clicked wetly into place.

Carl LaFaro, only fifteen years old, lay in the drive between the garage and the house. He had on only green thongs and white shorts, but the whole of his body was bright red, his belly opened from navel to throat, pink and grey loops of gut spread out to either side. His eyes and mouth were wide open.

"Fucken hell," Scott said, and turned to one side, vomited noisily. His dentures hit the dirt with his spew, but he barely noticed. He spat, and staggered on, heard more screams from the back of the house, another gunshot.

The front door stood open and Scott headed for it, not looking again at poor Carl as he hobbled past. When he got to the door he saw right through to the back door and Brennan LaFaro stood framed in it. He recognised the man's silhouette by its size and shape. "Brennan! Brennan, what the fuck?"

"Leave her alone!" Brennan screamed, then levelled a .303 rifle and fired again.

Scott ran through the house, his knees singing with pain at the abuse, as Brennan ran out into the back yard. Natasha LaFaro ran past him into the house, crying, the young girl's face ashen white. "It's killing everyone!" she screamed.

"What is?" Scott demanded. His heart hammered so hard in his chest he thought he might not get another three steps before a cardiac arrest ended him.

He got to the back door and saw the biggest red

kangaroo of his life, and he'd been around a while and seen a lot of reds. It was insanely muscular, over seven feet tall and it wasn't even stretched to its full height. Even in the bright midday sun its eyes blazed with orange fire. It held Cindy LaFaro by her shoulders, her feet thrashing two feet off the ground. She was bleeding from several places, her eyes wide and wild as she screamed.

"Leave her alone!" Brennan said again. He ran around the roo, trying to get broadside to it, his rifle levelled. But the roo turned on the spot, holding Cindy up like a shield.

"What the hell...?" Scott managed, skidding to a halt right outside the back door.

Brennan moved closer, the rifle shaking in his hands, no doubt from the man's combined fear and fury. "Put her down, ya fucker!" he yelled. He brought the rifle to his shoulder and aimed along it, the barrel raised.

Scott stared. Was he going for a head shot? Surely he'd hit his wife. The roo stood taller, impossibly tall, and tipped its head back in a kind of howling roar. Its mouth opened too wide, forested with rows of sharp teeth that had no place in a roo's face. Its extensive muscles bulged and flexed. Cindy LaFaro screamed, higher and louder than before. With a wet tear, the roo ripped both her arms out from the shoulders. Blood arced to either side as Cindy fell to the scrubby grass of the back lawn. She thrashed and wailed as blood jetted across the dirt, then she jerked violently once and lay still.

"Muuuum!" Natasha screamed from somewhere behind Scott.

Brennan yelled incoherent noises and fired. The roo flinched but didn't go down. Had Brennan missed?

The roo deftly switched its grip on Cindy LaFaro's arms, grabbed one bloody stump in each hand, and moved forward. It twisted left and right, whipping the disembodied arms side to side. The slack hands slapped across Brennan's face and head with fleshy thwacks and the man staggered backwards. His rifle swung loosely at his thigh as he stumbled groggily sideways, half insensate from the blows. The roo twisted left and right again and again, battering Brennan bloody with his wife's dismembered arms. Scott stared, unable to believe what he was seeing, frozen with horror and shock and impotence in the face of such insanity.

Brennan LaFaro collapsed to his knees. Valiantly, he tried to groggily bring the rifle up again to bear, but the roo leaped, almost vertically, some dozen or more feet high. It came down on Brennan's chest and shoulders, slammed the man into the grass where he flattened and burst like a dropped melon. Blood, bones, organs all splayed out in sudden, dismaying technicolour.

Natasha screamed.

The roo turned, twisting its huge feet in the mess that had until recently been Brennan LaFaro, and looked directly at Scott Moses. Scott pissed himself, vaguely stunned it hadn't happened until that moment. The roo, still holding Cindy LaFaro's arms, came towards him slowly. It put its front paws down, dragging Cindy's hands over the grass, pressed its thick tail to the ground and swung its back feet through in one lazy double-step forward.

Scott looked over his shoulder. "Run, Natasha!"

She stood halfway down the hall, her entire body vibrating in terror.

"RUN!"

She turned and bolted. Scott looked back at the

advancing roo and pulled the back door shut, hoping he might buy her enough time to get a head start at least. He pressed his back against the door. He felt terrible for what his daughter and her family would arrive to. Maybe they wouldn't come, after all. He thought of Marsha, hoped that, if nothing else, he'd get to see her again soon. "Please let there be something after this," he said, his voice weak.

He heard a car start on the other side of the house and its wheels spin in the gravel of the driveway, then it roared away. *Huh*, he thought absurdly. *Natasha must have got her driver's licence.* She was seventeen now, after all.

"Good for you, Tash," he muttered.

The roo stood up, dropped Cindy's arms, and took a casual hop to land right in front of him. He turned his head away from its hot, sulphurous breath and the roo's sharply clawed front paws closed over his shoulders. It pulled him into an agonising headlock and began to squeeze and squeeze.

9

Pat McDonough's hands shook as held the wheel. He tightened his grip, knuckles going white. Kealan got off the call to the police. "What'd he say?"

"Says he'll come as soon as possible. Said he'll have to call Federal Police if it's a murder."

"What did you tell him?"

"That we have no idea if it's a murder or not. He said he'll come out first and decide what to do."

"How long?"

"Fuck knows. He didn't say."

Pat shook his head. "I wonder what that useless fucker might consider an actual emergency."

They drove in silence for a moment, then Pat grabbed his phone, dialled.

"Big fine and five demerit points for that these days," Kealan said.

"You just told me the only copper for fucken miles isn't gonna be here any time soon."

"Good point."

Pat listened while Sheila's phone rang at the other end. When she answered he heard the rattle of the tractor in the background. "You talk to John?" she asked, without bothering to engage in pointless hellos.

"No, he wasn't there. But that salesman, Stred, he was there. And he was dead."

There was silence but for the tractor for a moment, then that engine went silent. "What did you just say?"

"John's not there, Stred is dead. We're heading back to town. I don't know what to do, Sheils."

"You call the bloody police, Patrick!"

"We did that, but who knows when he'll get here. You said a lot of people haven't been showing up for work and stuff, right?"

"I did."

"And now this."

"Something is up in Morgan Creek, that's for sure."

"We're heading to the pub, maybe you should meet us there."

"I'll call the CWA members. You call in any men you can think of. We need to start checking on people."

In the last few minutes into town, Kealan rang around. They stopped at the town's only servo, a small two-pump shack with a cracked cement apron and sagging wide-V roof, and jumped out to talk to SD Vassolo. No one knew what SD stood for and it had become a town gag, everyone offering suggestions. SD said if anyone ever guessed it right, he'd admit it and that person would get free petrol for life. But everyone still paid for their petrol in Morgan Creek.

Once they'd given a quick overview of events, Pat said, "SD, we're gathering at the pub, have a think about what to do. You want to help?"

"Of course." SD had a European accent Pat could never quite place. He pulled a filthy red baseball cap over his thick, greying curls, and stepped out, locking the servo shop door behind himself. He jumped up into the tray of Pat's ute and they drove the last bit into the middle of town and parked in front of the George Hotel, beside Kealan's wife's car.

A couple of people were standing around outside the pub.

"Thought you were going to leave us to dehydrate," Colin Mawber said as Kealan opened up, his smile bright in his dark face. A thick mop of black curls hung almost over his eyes.

"You seen Rich Duncan today?" Kealan asked. He hadn't been able to raise Rich on the phone, and Colin helped on the man's farm.

"Yeah, he's on his way in. Said we'd meet here."

"What about Charlie Rutledge? Couldn't raise him either."

"Haven't seen him, nah."

"I saw him just before dawn," SD said. "He stopped in and filled up, said he had to get to the workshop early to use the landline there to call his brother in America."

"Before dawn?"

"Yeah, time zones and shit, I suppose."

"What were you doing at the servo before dawn?" Pat asked.

"Tanker came and filled up my reserves. They drive at night sometimes, so I'm their first stop. I get there early to help 'em out. Means they finish their run before it's too late in the evening."

Pat turned to Kealan, but the man was already on his phone. He held up a finger as he listened. Then he shook his head. "Charlie's not answering his mobile or his shop's landline."

Rich Duncan pulled up and Pat felt a ripple of relief. At least one person unaccounted for seemed to be okay. "Let's walk around to Charlie's and check."

"The fuck you expect to find?" Bill Catter asked, strolling up and casting a wistful look at the pub.

The sound of the locks undoing made everyone turn, then the pub doors swung open.

"What the hell is going on?" Helen Burke asked.

Kealan gave his wife a quick rundown, then she agreed to open up the pub and wait for others while the men went around to Charlie's workshop.

"Fuck walking in this heat though," Rich said.

Shane Keene came along the footpath, his eyes concerned. "You sounded weird on the phone," he said to Kealan.

"We're going to check on Charlie."

Pat McDonough, Kealan Burke, SD Vassolo and Colin Mawber piled into the cab and tray of Pat's ute. Rich Duncan, Shane Keene and, reluctantly, Bill Catter squeezed into the front of Rich's ute. As they pulled away, Pat saw Tracy Robinson walking towards the pub. She and Helen fell into conversation, then he was turning past the Post Office and Real Estate office and heading towards Charlie's place a couple of blocks along.

As the two cars pulled up and the men all tumbled out, a loud bang echoed from somewhere across town.

"Someone's shooting," Kealan said.

"Fucken rabbits, prolly," Bill Catter said.

There was a moment of uncomfortable quiet, looks exchanged. They all jumped at the sound of another shot.

"Let's look in here first, then think about that," Shane Keene said.

Colin Mawber staggered back from the side door of Charlie's workshop, incomprehensible words falling from him. He pointed. The workshop had a big double roller door at the front, operated on a motor from inside. A smaller, regular door stood beside those. It had been open when they pulled up, Pat recalled. Colin had obviously gone for a look.

"What is it?" Kealan asked.

"Fucken look!" Colin Mawber said. His deeply dark face had gone the shade of ash.

The others went in. A single large roller door at the back of the workshop was open, flooding the large space with light. Two four-post automotive hoists took up most of the room, service pits beneath them. The place smelled of metal and oil. A small car was up on one lift, Tracy Robinson's little white Suzuki Pat noticed absently. The other lift was down and empty.

Between them was a red mess that used to be Charlie Rutledge. He was battered and bruised, a blood-soaked wrench held loosely in one hand where he'd clearly tried to fight off his assailant. The wrench had short, tan or ginger hair on it, Pat saw, stuck in the dried blood. But most of the blood by far was all over the floor by Charlie's ruined hip, filling the space where his left leg should be. Of his left leg there was no sign. The man's face was twisted in a rictus of pain and fear. He was very clearly long dead.

Oil cans and tools were scattered around the floor near where the back door had been rolled up, clearly marking the epicentre of their struggle.

"Fuck me dead," Bill Catter said. "His hoist fall on him or something?"

That possibility was so obviously not the case that everyone stopped and stared at Bill a moment.

"Fucken what?" he demanded, looking around at them all. "Which one of you pricks is Sherlock Holmes then? Got a better idea? His leg just fell off, did it?"

"Someone is violently attacking people in this town," Kealan Burke said.

"Someone or something," Pat said. "A lot of people are unaccounted for too. We need to figure out what the hell is happening here."

"Let's get back to the pub," Kealan said. "We tried to call around, and Sheila is gathering the CWA to meet there too. We can meet up and decide what's next."

"CWA?" Bill Catter said. "What? Are they gonna fuck knit a solution for us? Or bake some cherry fucken slice to feed the dead?"

"Stop being a cunt," Pat said. "Women are usually pretty level-headed in my experience. We need all the help we can get."

"Level-headed?" Bill said with a snort.

"Your own wife left you, Bill," Shane Keene said. "Can't get much fucken smarter than that."

Electric tension suddenly filled the garage as Bill turned on the older man.

"Enough!" Pat snapped, his voice harsh in the echoing service bay. "Everyone back in the cars and we'll have a beer and a chinwag about his. All of us, together. This is no time for fucken arguments."

"Sorry," Shane said. "You're right." But he didn't direct the apology, or even a look, at Bill Catter.

They climbed into the two utes and drove back around to the pub. As they pulled up side by side out the front of the George Hotel there was a screech of tyres and a blue Mazda 3 came careening around the corner. The terrified face of a young girl could be seen as she hunched over the wheel.

"That's Natasha LaFaro," Rich Duncan said as the girl drove directly into the back of Helen Burke's car in her panic. She vanished behind the sudden whiteness of the airbag.

10

Helen Burke came running out of the pub as Pat and the others reached Natasha's car.

"What's happening?" Helen said, skidding to a halt.

Pat pulled open the driver's door and Tash lurched away from him, screaming.

"It's okay," Pat said. "You're okay. Are you hurt?"

"Fucken 'roo, massive fucken 'roo killing everybody!"

"What?"

People exchanged worried looks as Pat helped the terrified girl out. She stood, looked around groggily. Her eyes were stretched wide, stark white in her tanned face. Her whole body vibrated with shock or fear, Pat couldn't tell which. Maybe both.

"A roo?" Shane Keene asked.

Tash flinched.

"You're okay," Pat said again. But he wondered if maybe he was lying to the girl.

"Fucken massive, fucken teeth and eyes like fire. Ripped mum's arms off, clean fucken off! And Dad!" Tash devolved into wracking sobs and slumped into Pat's arms.

He nearly fell, her dead weight dragging on him, but Kealan Burke grabbed her from the other side. "Let's get her inside. Shane, can you guys move her car?"

"I'll do it," Colin Mawber said. He glanced back the way she'd come, then climbed into the Mazda, pushing the deflated airbag out of his way. Shane stepped up to help, checking the damage to Helen's Ford.

"Worry about it later," Helen said. She held the pub door open and Pat led Tash inside, with Kealan's help.

Natasha mumbled and cried, shaking like she had a palsy. Kealan poured a large tumbler of whisky and handed it over. She just stared at it. Pat took the glass, tapped Tash on the chin.

"Open up," he said.

She seemed to suddenly realise the intent, and took the glass. She tipped it up, swallowed the lot in one and held the tumbler out to Kealan. Without a word he refilled it. Tash swallowed that one whole as well. Her trembling eased a little, her wild eyes softening slightly.

Shane and Colin came back in, SD, Rich Duncan and Bill Catter close behind. Tracy Robinson leaned on the bar, eyes narrow. As Tash looked from face to face, the pub door opened and Sheila McDonough came in.

"What's happening out there?" she asked. "Who crashed? You Tash?"

The young girl started crying again but it was a calmer emotion, less panicked. Sheila sat and put an arm around her shoulders. Carol Monroe from the café came in, then Sharon Duncan with Mindi Snyder, Sadie Hartmann, Amanda Spedding and Cassie Daley. Sharon went to stand beside Rich, put an arm around his shoulders.

"All the CWA I managed to raise at short notice," Sheila said, glancing around the women with a nod. "A lot of people aren't answering their phones."

"Charlie Rutledge is dead," Bill Catter said, carelessly.

Eyes swung to him, various glares, and Tash sobbed loudly again.

"They're all dead!" she said, voice high.

"Who, sweetheart?" Sheila asked.

"Everyone! Mum, Dad, Carl, even Mr Moses from

next door, I'm sure."

"Scott Moses?" Rich asked. "I was only talking to him yesterday arvo. The old bloke..." He trailed off into silence.

"What were you going to say?" Kealan asked. "The old bloke looked fine? I'm sure he was. Something is fucked around here."

"It's a massive red kangaroo," Tash said flatly.

They turned back to her again and she returned their gazes with defiant eyes.

"A roo?" Sheila asked.

"A massive fucken red. I'm not joking, never seen one so big." She held up the tumbler to Kealan again and he brought the bottle back over, refilled it. She sank it in one gulp, eyes glazing for a moment. Pat thought maybe drinking herself into a temporary oblivion wasn't such a bad idea. Hell, he'd like to do it himself.

"A roo is killing people?" Colin Mawber asked.

Tash nodded, swallowed. "It's huge, way bigger than my dad."

"Brennan LaFaro is six-three," someone muttered.

"Much bigger than my dad," Tash clarified. "It's the muscliest fucker I ever saw, its hands are huge, the claws longer than my fingers. And its back feet are fucken mental. Its middle claw is longer than this!" She pointed to her wrist and dragged a shaking index finger to her elbow."

"Don't be fucken daft, girl," Bill Catter, his tone derisive. "How the fu—"

Tash surged from her seat, raising her empty glass like she was about to smash it in his face. Kealan caught her arm and she strained against him.

"You think I don't know how fucken mental this sounds?" she screamed. "You think I'm making this shit up? It ripped Carl open. It tore my mum's fucken arms off! It stamped my dad into the fucken dirt! He shot it. I saw him shoot it, I'm sure he didn't miss, and it didn't even flinch. Its eyes are like flames and it has this wide mouth full of sharp teeth." She slumped and Kealan relaxed his grip and guided her back to sit between Pat and Sheila. "I know how all that sounds," Tash said, suddenly deflated. "But I'm not lying."

Silence hung heavy in the pub for a time. Kealan went behind the bar and lined up shot glasses. He poured whisky into each and said, "Come and get it. I think we all need it."

Every one of them took him up on his offer.

"What the fuck do we do?" Tracy Robinson asked.

"Hunt it and fucken kill it," Bill Catter said. "If what she says is true, we gotta kill the cunt."

"He's right," Shane said reluctantly. "Whatever it is, we gotta kill it."

"You all saw Charlie," Rich Duncan said. "We can't let it go on."

"Lot of people missing," Sheila said quietly.

"Your mob know anything about this?" Catter asked Mawber.

The young man turned, his eyes wide. "You fucken kiddin'? Don't sound like blackfella stuff to me."

"What the hell does it sound like?" Pat asked.

Mawber laughed. "Fire for eyes, sharp teeth, indiscriminate murder? Sound like whitefella business, you ask me."

"Fuck you!" Catter said, taking a step toward Mawber.

"You wanna try me, fucker?" Mawber said, standing tall.

"Calm down, everyone!" Sheila's voice was a whip crack and everyone turned. "Calm down," she said again, more quietly.

"What makes you say whitefella business?" Shane asked.

"Mate, have you read your people's fucken bible?"

The pub door opened and Steve Gomzi walked in, uniform shirt open at the neck. He took off his wide brimmed police hat and looked around the group, ran one hand over his balding head. "The fuck is going on here then?"

Five minutes later the cop was up to speed, drinking a shot of whisky with the others. He pursed his lips in thought.

"You gonna tell us this is police business and we should stay out of it?" Pat asked.

Gomzi's eyebrows shot up. "Fuck nah, get fucked!" He absently patted the pistol holstered on his hip, then looked around the group. "I need to file all kinds of reports and investigate these bodies you've told me about. But I think first we find and kill this thing." He looked at Tash, lips twisted. "A fucken roo?"

She stared back, face defiant.

"Fuck me dead." Gomzi looked around the group again. "How many of youse are armed?"

"Got a .303 in the ute," Shane said.

"Got my shottie in mine," Pat said.

"Registered or not?" Gomzi asked.

Shane's eyebrows knitted together. "Really, Steve? Now? You're worried we're gonna kill a murderous fucken roo with an unregistered gun?"

Gomzi nodded. "Sorry, force of habit. I've got a shottie too, in the paddy wagon."

"If I drive back home I can pick up two more .303s," Rich said.

"You blokes think maybe Pauline was the first victim?" Bill Catter said.

Everyone turned, surprised at the non sequitur.

"What's that?" Sheila asked.

"She left four or five days ago, that's what everyone thought," Bill said. "Maybe she didn't leave me."

"She fucken left you, you miserable shit," Kealan said. "We're only surprised she didn't leave earlier. You really hoping some massive feral fucken roo ate her, because that might mean she didn't fuck off on ya?"

"Fuck you!" Bill snapped.

"Nah, fuck you!' Kealan snapped back.

"Gentlemen," Sheila said, like a primary school teacher warning her class to settle down.

Silence hung for a moment, then Bill said, "I've got a .22 in my ute."

Steve Gomzi sniffed, standing up. "Right. I suppose it's up to me to make the plan, so here it is. The women can wait here, use the pub as a kind of home base. See who they can reach, offer help where they can. Everyone with a weapon, get it and meet out front in fifteen minutes. Then we hunt this bastard, whatever it is." He paused, then looked at Colin Mawber. "Can you track it?"

Colin's face twisted in disgust. "Because I'm black? We're not fucken born trackers, you racist fucker. I'm a cow hand."

Gomzi patted the air with both hands. "Didn't mean anything by it, just not sure how... bush... you... are."

"Fuck me," Mawber said. "Youse fuckers." He looked around, no one quite meeting his eye. "But," he said, eyes daring anyone to speak. "My cuz is a tracker. He works for the national parks service up in the Territory, and he's here visiting my mum." He pulled out his phone, glaring around the room. No one dared say a word. "You all shut the fuck up!" Colin barked.

Everyone made faces and noises of calm reassurance as Mawber dialled.

"Cuz," he said. "You at the house? Yeah, cool. Bring Dad's rifle and come to the pub right now, ey? I'll explain later." He hung up and looked around. "He'll be here in about ten minutes."

"Okay," Gomzi said. "Let's get organised."

11

Sheila McDonough looked around at the concerned faces in the quiet pub. It seemed strange without the men in it. Usually only a handful of women bothered to come into the drunkard's lair, as Sheila like to call it. The thieves' den. She enjoyed a visit quite often, though, the burly idiots didn't put her off. She wondered if this might not be the first time some of these women had ever been inside the town's central building. Tracy Robinson leaned on the bar, watching quietly. Sitting in a rough circle around Sheila were Sharon Duncan, Helen Burke, Carol Monroe, Mindi Snyder, Cassie Daley, Sadie Hartmann, and Amanda Spedding.

Sheila felt a need to rally them, lead them somehow, but had no idea where to start. It was one thing to be in charge of the CWA. This was entirely different.

"My old man didn't come home," Amanda Spedding said suddenly.

"Eddie didn't come home? From where?" Sheila asked, glad of something to break the silence, though the news did not bode well.

"He went for a game of cards with a few mates last night. Didn't come home."

"You rang?" Sharon Duncan asked.

"Of course. Sometimes he drinks too much, crashes there, comes home with his tail between his legs the next morning. But when I rang no one answered. Then you called, Sheila, so I came here."

Sheila nodded. "Lot of people gone missing in very

short order. Quiet town like this, news spreads fast, yet someone can be murdered in their own home and no one knows for days."

Amanda gulped back a sob. "You think Eddie's murdered?"

"I don't know what to think."

"We should get people safe," Tracy said. "Maybe suggest the town all come here, stay central until the beast is killed."

"Can it really be a murderous kangaroo?" Helen Burke asked.

Natasha LaFaro looked up from groggily staring at the floorboards. "S'true. But just cos it looks like a big fucken roo, who knows what it really is."

She slurred her words, the quick shots from earlier sinking in, but Sheila thought maybe she'd hit a nail on the head. But also, it was a fairly irrelevant nail. "Whatever it is," she said levelly, "it's killing a lot of people. The men will hopefully stop it. We need to try to protect the town in the meantime. Perhaps gathering everyone here isn't a bad idea, but we can't fit the entire town in the pub."

"What's left of the town," Sadie said quietly.

"There's room upstairs," Tracy said. "We've got a few hotel rooms, and the big reception room up there. Plus all this space. We can at least offer people sanctuary. If it overflows, we pick another place nearby."

"I'll stay here," Helen Burke said. "Keep the pub open and serve drinks to any who need 'em. I can get food going too."

"I'll go back to the café," Carol said. "Same reason. I'll make sure there's coffee and food for everyone if we use the pub as a gathering place. I'm too old for any other shenanigans anyway."

"And then what?" Cassie asked.

"Door knocking?" Mindi suggested.

Sheila pursed her lips, then nodded. "We need to be methodical. Ring around people and tell them to come here. Anyone who doesn't answer, we go and knock. That can only really work for the houses in town. Anyone out on the farms who doesn't answer… Well, I suppose they take their chances for now."

"One thing about that," Sadie said, and Sheila thought the woman looked contrite.

"About what?"

Sadie took a deep breath, then plunged ahead. "Something Bill Catter said has put me on edge. He was asking about Pauline, wondering if she was already killed?"

"Pauline finally got wise and got out, didn't she?" Tracy asked.

Sadie shook her head. "I'm not so sure. I run the book club, you know that, half of you come along. Well, last week after everyone left it was just me and Pauline Catter. She was dillydallying and I laughed and said, 'Don't you want to go home?' Well, she just collapsed into tears. Bill…" Sadie looked around the group, wary.

"Bill hits her," Sheila said flatly. "And more. I think we all know that. Maybe we've all consoled her from time to time as well, hmm?"

There were several nods and downcast eyes.

"Not that unusual, is it?" Helen Burke said. "Pretty common, especially out in places like this. Not Kealan!" she added quickly. "He's never raised his voice in anger at me, let alone a hand. But it happens."

"Of course, and we do what we can," Sheila said. "Pat and I certainly brought our boys up to respect women, and hopefully they do. Most are good, but there's bad apples everywhere."

"But Pauline was scared to go home," Sadie said. "I told her she could stay with me if she wanted to, but she was scared to do that too, because it would make Bill angry. Anyway, we had a couple of drinks, Dutch courage for going home she called it. It hurts less when she's drunk, she told me."

"That's sad as hell," Tracy muttered, and no one contradicted her.

"But I told Pauline, after a drink or two, that she should really consider leaving Bill. She needed to protect herself. And she said, 'Where would I go? Got no family to take me in. Got no money.' She's got no one." Sadie looked down, shook her head. "So she has to go back home. She's trapped there."

"But maybe it got too much and she took her chances anyway," Sheila said.

"Or she got taken by… whatever it is out there," Natasha said sleepily.

"She told me something else, though," Sadie said, looking around the group again. "She said she'd found an old mine shaft on their property. Most of it was fallen in, apparently, but a lot was still accessible. She said she sometimes goes there just to get away from Bill."

Various mutters and shaking of heads went around the group.

"You think she might be there?" Sheila asked.

Sadie licked her lips. "I don't know. I think maybe Bill hurt her too much and she's dead up there. Or maybe not. I also think there's more to that mine. As soon as she brought it up, after a few drinks, she became tight-lipped. Looked at me like she'd said too much. I asked her more about it, but she wouldn't say any more, then she hurried home. Said Bill would be angry if she was late. I haven't seen her since. Maybe she's stuck down there? What if she went to hide in there and some of it fell in on her or something. She might be hurt."

"Bill's out with the other men," Sharon Duncan said. "Someone should check on their place, see if Pauline's there."

"In the house and this mine," Sheila said. "Do you know where it is, Sadie?"

"Under the gum trees at the top of the north paddock, she said."

Sheila stood, motivated to act. "Okay, here's the plan. Helen and Carol at the pub and café respectively to take care of any townsfolk who come in. Can you two ring around town as well?" Both women nodded.

"I'll stay here too and help Helen," Tracy said.

"Good-o. Mindi, Cassie, Amanda, you three liaise with Helen and Carol, and you go and knock on any doors of people not answering their phones. Meanwhile, I'll go with Sharon and Sadie to the Catter property and we'll see if Pauline is anywhere to be found. We can stop in on the other farms along the way. Meanwhile, let's hope those men find and kill whatever's causing all this trouble."

She strode from the pub, energised by the need to do something, anything. She heard Sadie and Sharon follow her.

"We can take my car," Sadie said.

12

Matt Summers held the pliers tight as Michael Hicks screwed in another eyelet. The grass was yellow under his worn boots and Matt shook his head to dislodge a bead of sweat from this brow. Flies harassed his ears. The sweat hit the dirt and soaked in instantly. *This fucken drought.* The way things were going it would kill them all. Morgan Creek was slowly wasting away.

"Turn it in," Michael said.

Matt wound the pliers, tightened the turnbuckle to draw the fence wire taut.

"That's it," Michael said. "Another one done." He looked up along the line of fencing they were fixing and rolled his shoulders. "Reckon we'll get this bastard done before the end of the day?"

"Nah yeah," Matt said. "Knock on, ey."

Michael nodded and the two men trudged back to the ute parked up behind them, got another roll of wire, more clamps and pins and buckles.

"What the fuck even went through here?" Matt asked.

Michael shrugged. "No fucken idea. My stock weren't even in this paddock, had 'em north." He jabbed his own pliers back over his shoulders.

"I thought you must have had yer stud bull in here or something, and it tried to get next door."

Michael sniffed, shook his head. "Must have been something as big though, to rip out this much wire." He pushed his hat back, revealing a red and sweaty forehead, looked Matt in the eye. "You know what I reckon it really was?"

"What?"

"Rich fucken Duncan."

Matt frowned. "Rich? Why? And for that matter, how?"

"His farm is a few Ks that way, right?"

"Yeah."

Michael gestured back towards town. "And when he's not at his farm, he spends most of his time at the George Hotel, which is that way."

"Along with most of the town," Matt said. "You and me included."

"Nah yeah, I know. But Rich is there more, and for much longer. I reckon he decided on a short cut one night, and was too fucken drunk to notice this fence. He was heading for the gate over there, I reckon. Then he can follow the track to the south end of his place."

Matt barked a laugh. "You reckon he was pissed and drove straight through here and didn't notice?"

"Or didn't care."

"Yeah nah, Rich is a good cunt. If he noticed, he'd have told ya. Offered to help fix it." *I wish he had*, Matt added silently to himself. *Then I wouldn't be out here sweating my balls off*. "Should ask him," he said aloud.

"I will, count on it. Come on."

Michael cut away more broken fence wire and the two men set to replacing it with fresh. As they worked, Matt heard a whumping sound, somewhere behind. They were both bent over, pulling wire to tension, and when he tried to look back, he couldn't turn far enough to see.

"The fuck is that noise?" Michael said, right as Matt opened his mouth to ask the same thing.

The new fence wire forgotten, both men straightened and turned. They let out matching cries of alarm.

"Jee-fucken-zuss CHRIST!" Matt yelled, as the biggest red roo he'd ever seen surged towards them. It hit the ground with thundering slams, red dirt bursting up in clouds around its enormous back feet.

Matt staggered back, muttering oaths, as the huge, musclebound beast launched up over his ute. Michael backed up against the fencepost they'd been working on, five square inches of rough wood, silvered with age and sun, and watched the giant red as it rose higher and higher.

It's not going to clear him, Matt thought vacantly as the creature stretched down those huge feet and stamped into Michael's shoulders. Michael made a strangely loud *HURK* sound and slammed towards the ground, five square inches of old wood punching up and out through his chest. His ribs poked out around it like broken teeth and blood soaked the dry dirt.

"Fucken shit fucken shit fucken shit!" Matt staggered, ran randomly left and right, wondering where the hell to go in the wide open fields that seemed to stretch forever under an incandescent sun and the stupidly blue sky.

The roo stood beside Michael's staring body and slowly turned its head to gaze at Matt with orange flaming eyes.

"Nah nah nah," Matt gibbered. He turned to run and fetched up painfully against the side of the ute. His brain kicked in. Tearing his eyes from the impossible creature he leaned into the ute tray. When he turned back he had an Adler A110 All Weather Shotgun held level with his chest, its nickel-plated finish gleaming in the sun. He cranked the lever action, lined it up, and fired, less than three yards from the massive roo.

The animal flinched and staggered back. Matt blinked and looked away from a confusing burst of heat and light, working the lever action again. When he opened his eyes to bring the weapon up once more, the huge roo was right in front of him, standing tall over his five-eleven, heavy-set frame. The roo grabbed the barrel of the shottie in one giant paw, its fingers as long as Matt's, its claws the same length again at least, and wrenched sideways. The weapon boomed, but discharged off to the right, away from both of them.

The roo hauled back its free hand and punched Matt in the face with its long fingers outstretched, sharp, black claws puncturing in, rupturing flesh. Matt felt his skin flap open as searing pain washed through him and blood poured down his neck. He closed his fists and punched at the roo with all his might, battering it with both hands, but he might as well have been hitting a couch. The beast whacked him again, crosswise like a slap this time, and more of Matt's face shredded. He dimly registered his eyeball bursting, hot and gelid across his ruined cheek.

He hit the dirt, blood spattering it like rain, and rolled in time to see with his remaining eye the roo stretch up, then drop with both front legs outstretched, aiming for his head.

13

Three utes and a police paddy wagon pulled up
outside the LaFaro place at the edge of town and nine
people piled out, armed with a variety of rifles and
shotguns. The ruined body of Natasha's brother, Carl,
lay on the driveway. As the men approached, flies
swarmed up in a cloud and buzzed curiously around.

"What the fuck?" Jimmy Tennant said. Colin
Mawber's cousin crouched beside the corpse, his dark
face twisted in a grimace of disgust. He wore blue
cotton shorts and a t-shirt with the National Parks logo
on it. "A fucken roo did this?" He squinted back up at
the others, shaded his eyes with one palm.

"That's the story," Kealan said. "Natasha's back at
my pub swearing blind it's so."

"Come on," Pat said. "Let's get around the back."

They walked around the house, loosely two by two.
Colin Mawber and Jimmy Tennant in front, Kealan
Burke and Pat McDonough behind, then Rich Duncan
and Shane Keene, SD Vassolo and Steve Gomzi and
Bill Catter bringing up the rear.

"Shouldn't the fucken law be in front?" Pat called,
and Steve Gomzi frowned but jogged forward. He
drew his service revolver as he came and fell in
between Colin and Jimmy.

"Aw, get fucked!" Rich muttered as they came into
the back yard and saw the massacre across the scrubby
brown grass.

"That's Scott Moses over there," Shane said. "Or
what's left of 'im."

"Brennan's been fucken crushed, it looks like," SD

said.

"Went that way." Jimmy Tennant pointed across the yard to a three-wire fence that had been ripped apart.

"You sure that's not the way it came in?" Gomzi asked. "And now it's headed to town?"

Jimmy looked at the policeman with a furrowed brow. "This is whitefella policing, is it?"

"The fuck is that supposed to mean?"

"The fence is trailing out into the paddock, literally pointing the way, and we didn't pass a giant fucken feral roo on the way here, ya dipshit."

Gomzi bristled. "Don't you come the fucken raw prawn with me, mate!"

"Enough, both of ya." Pat pointed out across the paddock. "Can you track it?" he asked Jimmy.

"Probably." Without waiting for any further conversation, Jimmy strode off. The others trailed in his wake.

Jimmy seemed to have no trouble seeing the path the creature took, though Pat wondered if the man was simply following his nose. There were any numbers of marks and furrows in the scrubby field. They moved through two large paddocks, opened a gate into a third. Then Jimmy shielded his eyes again and nodded ahead.

"That a ute parked up there?"

"Looks like," Bill Catter said. "Matt Summers's old Toyota, I reckon."

"Your eyesight that good?" Kealan asked.

"Big fucken dent in the driver's door from when he had a bull think his car might make a good wife." Bill barked a throaty laugh, but the others didn't join him.

"Something lying in the grass by it," SD said.

"Or someone," Colin said.

The group approached more cautiously, all holding

their weapons a little more to hand. As they neared the ute, Pat saw that what lay in the grass beside the ute was a body, its head mashed to pulp. "That Matt?" he asked, turning to one side as he gagged.

"Yep," Bill said. "Recognise his overalls."

"Aw, fuck off," Rich said, turning away.

The others looked to see what had appalled the man and spotted Michael Hicks, arched unnaturally slightly off the ground, supported by a thick, square fence post punched right through his body.

"It definitely came this way," Jimmy said.

Silence hung heavy for a moment, then Pat said, "Ya fucken reckon, Jimmy?"

The group fell into hysterics for a moment, a pressure valve on their shock and fear finally giving way.

"All right, let's get our fucken ducks in a row," Steve Gomzi said. "Too many bloody dead cunts all over the fucken place. We gotta find this thing before anyone else gets hurt."

Jimmy pointed east. "That way."

They didn't question him, started to move on.

"Wait," Kealan said. "We're going a long way here, it's fucken mental to go on foot. Let's go back for the cars."

Bill Catter stood rubbing his chin, then pointed a little to the left of the direction Jimmy had indicated. "The Hightower farm is that way. We could drive straight there."

"Laurel Hightower wasn't at the pub," Pat said. "Sheila called in all the CWA, but she didn't come."

"Ah, fuck it," Shane said. He turned and started jogging as fast as his aging legs would carry him back across the paddocks towards the LaFaro place. The others matched his pace.

As the utes and Gomzi's paddy wagon skidded to a stop on the Hightower farmhouse driveway, the first thing they heard was screaming. Then the boom of a shotgun blast. They all piled out, started running.

"We really just blundering right into whatever that is?" Bill Catter yelled.

"We're not here to fuck spiders," Gomzi shouted back over his shoulder as the pack ran helter-skelter around the house.

Pat stuttered to a halt at the sight of the biggest red roo he'd ever seen. Despite the report from Natasha, and the recent evidence of its activities, nothing prepared him for what he saw. The beast stood well over seven feet tall, bulging unnaturally, even for a full-grown male red, with thick, corded muscle. Its face was split in a howl, its maw packed with sharp teeth, glistening red and hung with shreds of skin. Human skin. The two Hightower boys were torn to pieces beside the large hay shed. Their father backed away from the roo as it swung the limp corpse of Laurel Hightower by her feet. The man tried to bring his shotgun to bear again, but his wife's head arced around and cracked into his with a sound like two bowling balls colliding in a wooden alley. The middle-aged farmer dropped bonelessly to the dirt.

"Now let's finish that fucker!" someone yelled.

The other men were less stunned than Pat and started firing.

The roo dropped the body of Laurel Hightower and staggered back under the assault of multiple strikes of .303, .22 and shot. Everywhere a bullet struck, the red fur flew but no blood followed. The roo's eyes were burning orange flames. It lowered its head and hunched, and more flames burst from every hole a bullet had made, its body a forest of jetting fire.

Then the roo rose back to its full height, unharmed.

"Get the fuck fucken fucked that ain't no fucken roo!" Jimmy Tennant said, and bolted back around the house.

Pat could hardly blame the man. He wasn't armed and weapons seemed to do no damage anyway. After all that, armed to the teeth, they were useless.

"The fuck do we do?" Kealan Burke yelled, and all the armed men fired again. More flying fur, more bursts of orange fire, like mini jet engines through the beast's muscles, and then it came on again.

"Can we not fucken kill it?" Rich Duncan shouted. "What do we do if we can't fucken kill it?"

"We fuck off!" Steve Gomzi said, then fired five rapid shots from his pistol. "The bullets slow it, that's all."

Already the men were backing away in a tight group. The Hightowers were finished, and with no one to rescue, they could only save themselves.

"Follow it from the safety of cars and come up with a new plan," Pat said, finally finding the wherewithal to fire a shot of his own.

The giant beast hunched down, then leapt high. Yelps of alarm came from many throats as the monstrous animal easily covered the fifteen metres between them in a single bound. SD screamed as those two huge feet with their savagely long talons came down right on top of him. He crumpled beneath the creature's unnatural weight, bones snapping like kindling as he folded up. His arm spasmed out to one side and the police shotgun he held, given to him by Steve Gomzi, went off, both barrels. Gomzi's shriek was pure agony and horror as his groin and upper thigh disintegrated. Gore sluiced out of the remains of his police uniform pants like his gut was a bucket of offal that had been upturned. He fell, wailing.

The group of men split apart like they were water the roo had landed in. All but Kealan who tripped over SD's other arm, split and shattered across the red dirt. As Kealan went down on his arse, the roo turned and reached for him. Shane Keene quickly stepped back up, stuck the barrel of his .303 right under the roo's chin and fired. The animal's head flipped up, orange fire bursting out all around its muzzle. For a fraction of a second everyone paused, wondering if that point-blank shot might have finally finished thing. Gomzi's wails faded to silence. Then the roo's right arm, that had lifted with the attack, speared back down. Five long black claws punched into the top of Shane Keene's head and kept going. The man shuddered and shook violently as the roo's arm drove though his brain, then the beast grasped hold of something inside, lifted the old country store owner and swung him like a bat.

The man's limp body knocked Rich Duncan flying, but Shane's bravery had bought Kealan time to regain his feet. He caught Rich before the man could faceplant into the dirt and dragged him along. They stagger-ran back past the house to find two of the utes revving and turning in the driveway. Jimmy Tennant drove one and Colin Mawber the other.

"Get in!" both men hollered.

Kealan Burke and Rich Duncan dove into the tray of one ute, Pat McDonough and Bill Catter into the other, and both drivers floored it. The two battered old utes skidded and slewed side by side along the dirt driveway, took out the fence by the gate, and screeched onto the sealed road. Wind roared through Pat's hair as he looked back and saw the roo pulling Shane and SD to pieces.

Thank fuck it's not following, he thought to himself,

his entire body vibrating with shock. *Then again, why would it need to follow? We can't kill the fucker, it has all the time in the world.*

14

Sheila McDonough, Sharon Duncan and Sadie Hartmann arrived at the Catter property and sat in Sadie's car outside, staring at the weather-beaten farmhouse. Its weatherboards were split and peeling, the tin roof rusting, not unlike all their houses, if truth were told. The outback sun played havoc with civilisation, but she and Pat took pride in keeping their place fixed up, as would a lot of the families out here. She put the last coat of paint on their house herself, section by section in between the farm work one winter when it wasn't too hot to do the work.

A house was often a reflection of its occupants. And the Catter property was falling apart.

"Your Pat ever hit you, Sheila?" Sharon asked out of nowhere as Sadie killed the engine.

"Hell no. He'd come a cropper if he did and he knows it, I'd have no qualms about hitting him back. But he's not a violent man anyway. He gets angry, depressed too, it's hard out here, you all know that. But he never resorts to violence even when he's had a skinful, not like so many do."

Sharon nodded. "My Rich is the same. His dad was terrible violent, a drinker, used to beat his mother. Some men perpetuate what they see, but some promise never to be that way themselves. Thankfully that's Rich's position."

"My Josh might look like the south end of a north bound camel, but he's a good man too," Sadie said.

"He's not that bad!" Sheila said, but couldn't suppress a laugh.

"He is and you know it, but I bloody love him," Sadie said. "Face like a dropped pie," she added, grinning.

"Ugly as a hat full of arseholes," Sharon said, and all three devolved into brays of laughter.

"But the rest of him," Sadie said, getting her breath back. "Oh, he's lovely elsewhere and an expert with what he's got."

They settled a little and Sheila smiled at Sadie beside her, Sharon leaning through from the back seat. "We're lucky, us three," she said.

"We are. And so are our bloody husbands," Sharon said. "Don't forget that."

"Punching above their weight, all three of 'em," Sadie said with a grin.

Sheila nodded. "Most definitely. Such a shame so many women aren't so lucky. That many widowers around here because their women shot through. And no blame for that, either. So many more living with violence and abuse. It's not right." She stared out through the windscreen at the battered house while she spoke. "Should we have done more for Pauline?"

"Like what?" Sharon asked. "I've had her stay at mine a few times, so has Sadie. You've given her harbour in a storm often enough as well."

"But she kept going back!"

"She had no choice," Sadie said quietly. "Like she told me, no money, no family. And Bill would only be worse if she stayed away too long." Her eyes darkened. "We're bloody lucky, us three, but there's a few here and there I'd like to see get their comeuppance."

"We should have *kept* Pauline away from him," Sharon said. "Told him to fuck off."

"You expecting to find a body in there?" Sheila asked, laying a soft hand on Sharon's shoulder.

"We might."

"Come on then, we can't put it off any longer. Besides, this car's getting hotter than Satan's arsehole with the AC off."

The front door of the house was unlocked and the three women stepped warily into the hall. The place was stuffy from being closed up all day, but a little cooler than the scorcher outside.

"Strewth, Pauline keeps a tidy home," Sharon whispered.

She was right, the place spick and span, everything neatly in place, an aroma of lavender drifting lazily.

"You never been before?" Sheila asked.

"No."

"Me either," Sadie said. "I suggested having the book club here now and then, but she said Bill would never stand for it."

They moved cautiously through the house, speaking in low tones as though they were in a museum. Despite its cleanliness and order, the home was empty. Once they'd checked all three bedrooms, lounge room, dining room, kitchen and bathroom, Sheila manage to let out a small sigh of relief. It would have been terrible to find Pauline here and hurt at Bill's hand. Or worse still, dead. Then again, was it better if she'd been killed by a feral kangaroo? Could that really be what was happening around Morgan Creek? Please let it be the truth they'd all thought until now, that Pauline had finally found a way to get out.

You blokes think maybe Pauline was the first victim? Bill Catter had said.

Are you the only one allowed to hurt her? Sheila thought. *Or was Kealan on the money when he suggested you maybe hoped the roo had got her so it didn't mean she'd finally got up the courage to leave you? Damn you, Bill Catter, you make me mad as a cut snake.*

"She's not here, then," Sharon said, turning to Sadie.

Sadie nodded. "So we gonna check this old mine then?"

Sheila turned and strode from the house. "Come on," she called back over her shoulder. "Let's get to it. Lead the way, Sadie."

As they walked, Sharon asked, "What sort of a mine anyway?"

"Pauline told me that Bill told her it was an old gold mine," Sadie said. "This property has been in Catter hands for a few generations. Apparently Bill's grandfather had decided there might be gold on his land and had started a mine."

"There was never gold found anywhere near here," Sheila said.

Sadie shrugged. "Bill Catter wouldn't know a tram was up him until the passengers started getting out. Why should his grandfather be any different?"

"You're not wrong," Sheila said. "I knew Bill's father and that man was a few sangers short of a picnic too. Rough as a mile of country road, all the Catter men."

"It's a good reminder to teach our sons to be better than their fathers," Sharon said. "It starts with the kids."

"Again, you are not wrong," Sheila said.

Sadie stopped, shading her eyes against the glare of the setting sun. It was sinking slowly towards the distant hills, but still had the heat to burn the skin off milk. "That's Catter's north paddock. Pauline told me the mine shaft Bill's grandfather built was under the blue gums on the far side. That's all she said, 'Under the gums on the far side of the north paddock'."

Sheila pointed. "That way, by the looks of things."

"Come on then."

All three women had worked up a sweat by the time they got into the shade of the trees. It didn't take long to see the mine. A sun-bleached wooden shed stood incongruously under the dappled shade of gum leaves. It had a bent tin roof, peeled up at one corner by wind or maybe a falling branch in the distant past. Remarkable that it still stood at all, but they made things to last in those days.

They moved around it, looking nervously into the shadows under its twisted frame. Sure enough, a piece of wood had been pulled aside and a dark hole led into the rocky ground. Not a piece of wood, Sheila corrected herself, but an old section of paling fence. Weathered and worn, but much newer than the shed over it. Had Pauline dragged this up here?

Sheila moved closer to the hole in the ground – a neat square some two metres to a side – and peered in. It was smoothly dug, and a wooden ladder with wide rungs disappeared into the darkness. A sensation of cool air rose from it.

Sheila looked up at Sadie and Sharon, both leaning over either side of her to look down. They both shrugged at her questioning eyes.

"Pauline!" Sheila yelled into the hole. "You down there?"

She felt entirely stupid hollering into a hole in the ground out the back of beyond, but they had to be sure.

Then someone called back.

All three women jumped, startled, and stepped back. Sheila quickly moved forward again. "Pauline? That you?"

"Help me, please!"

The words were faint, weak despite being shouted. They sounded like they came from a raw throat. Had Pauline been trapped down here for days?

"Bloody hell," Sheila said, turning and quickly finding her footing on the ladder. She hurried down, Sharon and Sadie close behind.

15

As the two utes carrying the six men sped back into town, Pat noticed a few people in the streets, looking worried. The townsfolk had begun to catch on that something was amiss in Morgan Creek. No doubt several were also responding to the call and coming to seek shelter.

"Get to the pub!" Pat yelled from the ute tray. "Meet at the pub!"

People looked scared or sceptical, but they must have seen the blood on the men's faces, the rifles and shotguns in their hands, perhaps even the grief and terror in their eyes.

The two cousins skidded the utes to a halt outside the George Hotel and the six survivors of Hightower farm jumped out and ran inside. A decent number of people were already there, most drinking, the talk a loud hubbub that fell silent as the men piled in.

Helen Burke came running around the bar to hug Kealan, her eyes wide.

"Where are the others?" Tracy Robinson asked. "Where's Shane?"

Pat shook his head, lost for words.

"Cactus," said Bill Catter heartlessly. "So are Steve Gomzi and SD. Fucking monster roo, can't be killed."

Whispering and muttering rose, then shouted questions, all overlaying each other to make a white noise of angry voices.

Pat moved over towards Helen. "Where's Sheila?"

"She went with Sharon and Sadie to check on Pauline."

"Pauline Catter? Didn't she shoot through?"

"That's what they're checking, I guess."

Pat nodded, lips pursed. He glanced back at Bill, who didn't seem to have heard their conversation. Pat didn't like being away from his wife, but at least she'd gone in the opposite direction to the Hightower farm, and therefore hopefully the roo. He looked around at the shouting and arguing crowd in the pub. What a mess.

Kealan put two fingers in his mouth and blew a shrill whistle. The pub sank into silence again. "We need a plan," he said. He looked at Pat.

Pat startled, unsure what the man wanted from him. "I don't have a fucken plan," he said. He gestured vaguely back over his shoulder. "Honestly, the fuck are we supposed to do about that? We tried to kill it."

"We call someone in," Bill said. "Call the fucken army."

"And say what?" Rich Duncan asked. "Come with a tank, there's a killer fucken roo in the north paddock?"

Bill turned on him. "What do you suggest?"

"You got a fucken number for the army, have ya, Bill? One eight hundred fucken soldier, is it?"

Bill drew a fist back, ready to floor Rich, and Rich stood up to the man, face furious, but Jimmy Tennant grabbed Bill's arm. "Cut it out! You galahs having a blue in here won't fix anything out there."

"Back down, Bill," Kealan said. His eyes were dark and Pat thought the man was close to violence himself. The entire pub, he realised, was a powder keg of fury, built from fear. They needed direction.

"We do have to call for help," Pat said. "Steve Gomzi is dead, so perhaps we'd best start with trying to find the police and get them in. Who's closest, Broken

Hill?"

"They're fucken hours away," Rich said.

"Every cunt is fucken hours away from here," Bill said. "We need to fight this ourselves."

"How?"

"Just call triple-0 and get them to send all the cops they can," Kealan said. "In the meantime, we need to barricade ourselves somewhere safe and come up with a plan of defence."

Tracy raised her hand from behind the bar. "I'll do it." She turned and picked up the phone.

"How many more weapons can we get?" Pat asked. "And does anyone have anything… I dunno, bigger?"

A hand rose at the back and big Jim McLeod stood up. His thick ginger hair and beard reflected the light from the wall sconce above his head. "I've got some dynamite."

"Now you're fucken talking!" Bill said.

"Why the fuck have you got dynamite?" Pat asked.

"Was planning to blow up some of the rocks at the back of my place. I need more pasture."

Jim stared at Pat with defiant eyes, and Pat decided now wasn't the time to discuss the sanity of the man's idea. Or apparent lack of it. "Right," he said instead. "How much you got?"

"Few cases."

"Fuck me dead," Pat said quietly. Then more loudly, "Can you go and get it?"

"Bring it here?"

"Yep. I have no idea what we'll do with it, but it seems like the sort of thing we might appreciate having around."

"We can set a trap," Bill said. "Find somewhere to lure that evil fucker into, line it with dynamite, then blow the bastard to pieces."

"Might put you in there as bait, eh, Bill?" Jim McLeod said.

"Get a dog up ya!" Bill snapped.

"Enough!" Pat shouted. He looked over at Bill. *No one likes that shit cunt. Why have we ever put up with him this long?* Then again, what would they do? It wasn't like the wild west where they could simply run someone out of town. But maybe that's exactly what they should have done, years ago. "Jim, please go and get the dynamite."

"Righto." The big man shouldered his way past a few drinkers and went outside. The roar of his ute starting up shattered the silence and people began shouting and clamouring again.

Kealan Burke whistled them into silence once more. "Now we need to think about securing this place. I'm happy for people to use the pub to shelter, it's one of the biggest buildings in town and it's made of brick, but we won't fit everyone. Where else can people bunker down?"

"Police are coming," Tracy called out.

"What did you tell them?"

"I thought maybe mentioning a killer kangaroo might be tempting fate, they'd think I was mad. So I said there have been multiple murders in town and everyone is scared. I claimed no further knowledge."

"Smart. They say how long?"

"Nah. Just that they'd send someone right away."

"Fucken useless pack o'cunts," Bill Catter said. "What'll they do when they get here?"

There was silence again, and Pat knew people might not like Bill, but they couldn't help agreeing with him on that comment. Especially those recently returned from the Hightower farm. They'd seen firsthand how hopeless the situation was.

Kealan turned back to the crowd. "For now, let's

think of ways we can make this place more secure. And who else has buildings big enough for people to hide in?"

He didn't get an answer because everyone spun around at the sound of terrified screams.

"Oh, fuck," Pat muttered.

They crowded to the windows and saw people running down the street. At the far end, the huge red roo bounded into view, eyes ablaze.

"That's Mindi Snyder, Cassie Daley and Amanda Spedding at the far end," Tracy said. "They were going door to door around town to warn people."

"That's why so many people are here?" Pat asked.

"I guess."

Other people ran ahead, but those three women had nothing between them and the roo except about fifty metres of the main street. Kealan ran to the pub doors and opened them wide.

"Everyone inside, now!" he yelled, and the few people in the road bolted towards him.

"Use the cars!" Pat said suddenly.

"What?" Bill's expression was confused and derisive at the same time.

"Cars," Pat said again. "We've got heavy utes, they've all got steel bull bars. They're on the fucken things in case we hit roos on the road. Let's weaponise 'em!"

"Now that's a good idea," Kealan said.

Several townsfolk ran out and jumped into any car or ute with a heavy bull bar. Others ran past them into the pub as the cars revved and roared, tyres squealing as they peeled out of parking spaces.

Pat drove hard for the end of the street and saw the roo leap high and land right behind the three women running for their lives. He'd never reach them in time.

They sprinted right down the middle of the street, eyes wide in terror. Mindi on the left, Cassie on the right, and Amanda Spedding in the middle. As Pat stared, helpless, Amanda arched forward. Her face twisted in pain and a fraction of a second later the roo's long back foot punched out through her abdomen, strung with loops of intestine like profane glistening Christmas decorations. The other two women screamed and ran in opposite directions as the roo shook its foot free of Amanda's corpse. It looked left and right, and chose Cassie Daley next.

It sprang up, easily clearing the short distance she'd managed to run, and came down right beside her. She'd nearly made it to the Rose Boutique store. As she ran up the kerb, the roo leaned back on its thick muscular tail and thrust both feet forward. The huge limbs slammed into Cassie's back and launched her across the footpath. She slapped face first and dead flat into the bricks beside the shop door, blood bursting out all around her. Pat saw an eyeball and some teeth fly out to the side with the impact. She peeled back from the wall and fell like rags to the ground.

He floored the accelerator and drove headlong into the beast. His ute was a Toyota HiLux, nearly one and half tonnes of metal with a solid steel bull bar on the front. The roo turned as Pat bore down on him. Pat leaned hard over the wheel and yelled, "Fuck you!" and the car smashed into the creature. The impact rang the car like a bell, shockwaves made Pat's teeth rattle. It was as though he'd driven into a solid wall. His chest slammed into the wheel as the back end of the ute rose up. Metal screeched and groaned, steam burst up from the bonnet as the bull bar drove back into the engine bay.

The roo was thrown back from the car some five

metres, where it hit the asphalt and slid another two metres on its side. Gasping for breath, clutching his chest, Pat looked out at the inert beast. Had it worked? *Please, let the thing be dead.*

The roo flinched. Shook itself. Stood back up.

"Aw, fuck you!" Pat screamed. He tried to drive forward again, but the engine screamed and metal ground against itself. The car was useless. He stared at the roo and the roo stared at him.

Then Colin Mawber drove in across the road doing a maniac speed and collected the roo and kept going. The ute he drove picked up the roo on its bull bar even as the unnatural weight of the creature bent the bar back. But the ute kept going and slammed the beast right through the brick wall on the other side of the big window to where Cassie had died. Glass and bricks and dust rained down all over the cab of the ute, the roo vanishing into the wreckage.

Colin scrambled out of the passenger side as Pat leapt out of his own broken vehicle.

"Did it work?" Colin yelled.

"No idea," Pat called back. "Let's go!"

They began to run back towards the pub as the bricks and timber window frame shifted and fell, and the roo pushed its way out of the wreckage. Pat shook his head. What chance did they have against this monster? Nothing could kill it.

He and Colin ran and the roo bounced out into the middle of the road. Pat knew it could reach the two of them in only one or two more bounds and they were as good as dead already, but they sprinted on regardless.

Then Rich Duncan was speeding past them in his ute. He had the straight road in his favour and had to be doing a good 80kmh. Pat saw the man's face set in a rictus of grim determination, hunched over the wheel.

He couldn't help himself, slowing to turn and watch.

The roo saw the car coming and crouched, braced for the impact. *Come on*, Pat thought. *Kill that bastard*. Surely a massive car going that fast would finish it. He only hoped Rich would survive the high-speed collision.

At the last possible moment, the roo leaped. Pat's heart sank, he thought it was going to go clean over the car, but it didn't leap up, it went forward, short arms with their deadly claws out in front. It stretched its body flat and speared right through the windscreen. Right through Rich Duncan. Its massive tail split the car's roof open like a sardine tin as the roo's massive body punched through it and out the back screen. The beast landed on the road shaking blood and bones from its head and shoulders. A section of spine, soaked in blood, clacked onto the asphalt. Rich's ute ploughed on briefly before swerving out of control left, right, left again, then it tipped and rolled, smashing through a power pole which dropped and tore the power lines down with it. White and blue sparks leapt and danced on the road and all over the wreckage of Rich's car.

Pat saw Mindi Snyder cowering in a shop doorway only a few feet from where the roo had landed. The beast held Pat's eye for a moment, then turned to see what he was looking at. Just how smart was this monster? It hopped almost casually sideways and Mindi screamed as it plucked her from her supposed safety. It hopped back, holding her out in front of itself by her shoulders, like an offering. Pat frowned. Was it showing her to him? Showing off? Pat and Colin, side by side in the road, could only gawp in horror.

The roo's eyes blazed with orange fire and it lifted Mindi higher. It reached down and grabbed one ankle, then the other, flipping her over to hang upside down.

Mindi screamed and thrashed, but its grip was vice-like.

"Put her down!" Pat hollered uselessly.

The roo seemed to pause a moment, then it lifted Mindi higher still and drove her headfirst down onto the hard bitumen. Her screaming cut instantly short as her arms folded up and her head burst.

Pat stared, the only thought in his mind being thanks that Sheila was currently far away from here, at the Catter place. He hoped she stayed there. Then he and Colin turned and sprinted again for the pub.

16

Sheila crept along the cool dark mine passage, her phone held out in front as a torch. Sadie and Sharon followed, their own phone lights adding to the illumination. The mine was well-built, solidly supported with wooden beams. The initial shaft only went down about three metres, then levelled out into a tunnel. The tunnel began to slope gently downwards as they moved along, occasional side branches to the left and right.

Each of the side tunnels ended after only a metre or two, some unfinished, others fallen. Except one that went for maybe five metres before ending in a rough rock wall. Catter's grandfather had put in a lot of labour here, Sheila mused. The man was truly insane. As if he'd find gold in a place like this. Then again, maybe he had found something that made him think further digging was worthwhile. Perhaps there was opal in the rocks, and he'd shifted from thinking about gold to mining that. That rock wall they'd seen was a good candidate and it had shown several areas of chiselling and chipping.

"Pauline?" Sheila called again.

"Please hurry!"

The voice was stronger now.

"Definitely dead ahead," Sadie said.

The three women hurried on and a foul stench began to reach them.

"Smells like something died down here," Sharon said.

They emerged into a larger space and all shuddered to a halt. Body parts littered the floor. A leg here, arms there. Sheila saw a head and realised it was that guy Stred who came around selling farm supplies. The entire corpse of John Lynch lay propped up against one wall. Dozens more parts in various states of decay or dismemberment covered the rough ground.

"Oh, Jesus, why?"

Sheila realised it wasn't herself or Sadie or Sharon who had spoken. With a shaking hand she lifted the phone to cast the light to the back of the broad space and realised they were in a natural cave, with evidence of Grandfather Catter's mining here and there around the edges. And on the far wall, hanging in a complicated pattern of wooden beams, was Pauline Catter.

The woman's clothes were ragged, dirty and blood-spattered. Her feet just reached the floor, her arms out to either side in some parody of crucifixion. Her hands had been crushed between two wooden beams, one built into the wall, another dropped on top of it, to hold her in place. Her wrists were black bruises and angry red where they disappeared under the wood. *Her hand bones must be crushed to paste in there*, Sheila thought.

"Pauline, what the hell?" she cried, running to her.

"Don't move me!" Pauline said. "My hands!"

"I see. We have to get you out of there. Sadie, Sharon, help me!"

The three women moved to either side of their friend and tried to get a grip on the huge wooden beam that had Pauline trapped.

"What is happening here?" Sheila asked, scrabbling at the old hardwood for a grip.

"It's all my fault!" Pauline wailed. "I just wanted him gone. That bastard!"

"Who?"

"Bill, of course!"

Sheila stopped looking for a grip and stared at Pauline. "Bill did this?"

"No, no, that's not what I mean. I did it."

"You did it?"

Pauline nodded forward and Sheila turned to see an old steamer trunk. A large book sat open on its lid, an incredibly old looking book.

Sheila turned back. "Let's get you out of here first."

The three women tried again to shift the huge beam trapping Pauline, but it was too heavy for them to budge even an inch.

"Can we drag it forward?" Sadie asked.

"It'll fall on her if we do," Sharon said. "No way we can get it off and her out from under it at the same time. We need more people here. It'll take half a dozen of us or more to lift this."

"How long have you been here?" Sheila asked.

"Days. I don't know, it's always dark. I can only see when it comes back, its eyes are like torches."

Sheila furrowed her brow. "What did you say?"

Pauline hung her head and gasped in a sob, then looked up again. "You have to listen to me! I used to come down here to hide out. I found that old trunk in one of the side passages, I don't think Bill ever knew about it. It belonged to Percy Catter, Bill's grandfather. The man is certifiable, completely off his rocker, but he was well-travelled. He originally emigrated here from Romania, but he'd been all over before that. There's a journal in there, talking about the places he went. He spent a lot of time in Persia, as he called it. He talks about buying a book from a spice dealer, who told him it contained power over entities beyond our understanding. That book, on the trunk there. It's bound in human skin, Sheila, and written in blood."

"Pauline, please—"

"Fucken listen to me!" Pauline shouted, and Sheila dropped into a shocked silence. "I'm sorry, but his is so important. There's a bit in that book that talks about summoning the power of death. It says you can turn that death onto whoever you choose. And I wanted him dead, Sheila. I wanted Bill dead for the things he does to me."

Pauline devolved into sobs and Sheila stepped forward. She gently brushed back her friend's dark hair. "I understand, Pauline. Really I do."

"The ritual called for an animal sacrifice and I could never bring myself to kill something. Can you believe that? I was too squeamish about it. A farmer's wife and I even baulked at bringing a chook down here to slit its throat. Then I found a roo caught up on the fence not far away, torn up by the barbed wire. It was a male, a red, but not that big. And it was clearly dying, nothing I could really do to save it. It was weak and hardly moving. So I saw my chance. I quickly unhooked it and dragged it down here. I had to hurry before I lost my nerve, but I must have fucked up, done something wrong.

"The ritual seemed to be working, orange light and a godawful stink filled up the place. The roo started to twitch even though I'd just killed it. Cut its throat. The sacrifice, yeah? Then it started to… to fill out. It grew and grew, got taller and muscular and its eyes lit up with flames. Then it opened its mouth and that just got wider and wider and these long sharp fangs burst up, knocking the roo's normal teeth aside. I thought it was going to kill me, but it just stood there, staring.

"And here's where I fucked up, I think. There was other script in the book, a strange language I couldn't read, and I think maybe there was some instruction in there, some way to bring it to my will, make it do what

I wanted. But I frantically looked through, kept yelling at it to go away, I was so scared. I didn't know what I'd done, I hadn't expected anything like that. I just wanted to wish Bill dead." She sobbed again. "Eventually it grabbed me and hung me up here, so strong it had no trouble with that beam. Then it went away. I'd thought I'd be left here to die. But it kept coming back, bringing me… things. By the light of its eyes, I'd see more and more parts, so much blood…" She collapsed into tears again. "And it still hasn't even killed Bill, has it?" she wailed between sobs.

"We have to get you out of here," Sheila said. "Sadie, Sharon, come on. All your strength, girls, let's lift this bastard thing off her."

17

The George Hotel was a war zone. A screaming crowd huddled at the bar while Pat McDonough, Kealan Burke, Colin Mawber, Jimmy Tennant and Bill Catter stood in a rough semi-circle between them and the giant roo, firing rifles and shotguns. The ordnance was deafening in the confines of the buildings, the muzzle flashes only outshone by the orange fire jetting out of every wound they put in the roo, the flames closing each wound up again. Their firepower, strong as it was, barely held the monster back, and their ammo was nearly gone.

Several people hadn't managed to get clear as the huge beast had smashed into the front wall of the pub, then given up on the brick and burst in through one of the large plate glass windows. They'd barely had a chance to start upending tables to block access before the roo was inside and on them.

This is it, Pat thought. *Nothing can stop it. We're all dead.*

The roo grabbed one screaming patron by an arm and a leg, lifted him high and slammed him down onto an upturned table leg. The wood speared through the man's torso and he coughed up a spray of blood. Pat kept firing as the roo moved forward, grabbed two people trying to scramble away, and crushed them together, its massive chest flexing with the effort. The smack of their impact into each other was sickening.

Pat's rifle clicked empty. Bill stared in disbelief at his shotgun, now only any good as a club. Helen emerged from behind the bar holding Kealan's cricket bat.

The roo hopped forward again, its eyes two blazing furnaces. It leaned forward, staring hard at the semi-circle of men, head moving left and right as it scanned them. Pat thought he could feel the heat emanating from it. Then it cocked its head to one side, as though listening. It stood up tall, half-turned, twisting its torso to look back out the ruined window.

Then it shifted and leapt, clear across the pub and out through the hole where the window had been in a single bound.

"Where's it going?" Kealan asked.

They ran forward, dragged the tables away from the doors and opened them to look out. The roo was powering out of town, taking giant ten metre bounds.

"What's that way?" Jimmy Tennant asked.

Pat swallowed. "Among other things, your place, Bill."

Bill looked at him with a frown. "So what? Nobody's there. Good fucken riddance."

"My wife is there," Pat said. "And Sharon Duncan and Sadie Hartmann."

"What the fuck for?"

"Never mind why," Kealan said. "Come on. We have to get them out if we can."

"We'll clean up here," Colin Mawber said. "And use the time to barricade properly. Get back here and we'll have it as secure as possible. With any luck, by the time you get back, Jim'll be here with his dynamite." He threw a couple of boxes of ammo over. "That's all that's left.

Kealan caught the boxes. "Good man."

Pat, Kealan and Bill ran out and jumped into Helen Burke's car, the back end all dented in from Natasha's impact.

"Always leaves the keys in it," Kealan said with a grin, starting it up.

"This thing gonna work?" Pat asked.

"Let's see." Kealan put it into gear and backed out. It made some nasty grinding noises from the back, but whatever was dragging at the wheel cleared and Kealan turned the face down the road. They powered out of town and just caught sight of the roo in the distance. It was indeed heading directly for the Catter farm.

"Why is going to my place?" Bill asked. "And why is your wife there?"

"The women were checking on as many townsfolk as they could. Those three went out to look for Pauline."

"Yas all know she fucked off," Bill said, angry. "What, you think I got her tied up in there?"

Pat and Kealan both looked at Bill with dark eyes, saying nothing.

"Fuck all o'yas cunts!" Bill said. "She's fucken gone, I tell ya."

"Regardless, my wife is there with Sharon and Sadie, so we have to save them."

The roo moved at an incredible pace, and cut across country while Kealan had to follow the road. They lost sight of it for a time, then Kealan turned into Bill Catter's long drive and they saw the roo bouncing past the house, heading north. Kealan drove past the house as the roo leapt the fence and kept going.

"Fuck the car," Pat said. "Don't lose it!"

Kealan sped up again and drove right through the fence wires. Bill grimaced, but wisely kept his trap shut. The small car bounced and rattled across the rough paddock, shaking the men's teeth loose in their heads. The noise started up at the back again, worse than before, and the rear corner tilted downwards. They all held onto something, watching as the roo swerved into a patch of blue gums at the far side. It bounded over a small shed among the trees and vanished from sight.

"What the fuck?" Kealan said.

"An old mine shaft back there," Bill said. "I think it fell in."

"A mine shaft?" Pat asked.

"Long story. My grandfather was as useless as tits on a bull, had some mad fucken ideas."

Something metallic twanged and the car slewed sideways. Kealan yelled in surprise and fought it to a stop. Not delaying to worry about the damage, all three men jumped out and ran for the tatty shed. They stared at the dark, square hole in the ground. Then they heard screaming.

"Jesus fuck!" Pat yelled, and ran for the opening.

The others followed him and, as Pat started down the old wooden ladder, Bill said, "You're really going down there?"

"You hear the fucken screaming?" Pat demanded, and kept going.

He heard Kealan's voice above him. "Whatever this is, it's on your land, Bill. Take some responsibility, you shithead."

Pat hit the dirt at the bottom of the ladder and glanced up. Kealan and Bill were both following him down. They took out their phones, used the flashes to light the way. Screaming and shouting echoed up to them and in moments they came out into a large cave. Pat skidded to a halt. Sharon Duncan hung from the giant roo's front paws, one jammed into each eye socket. Her body was limp as a flag on a windless day. Pauline Catter hung from a wooden framework at the back of the cave with Sheila to one side of her and Sadie to the other.

Kealan and Bill ran up beside him as Pat lifted the .303 and fired. The roo's head whipped sideways, then fire shot out and it drew itself up tall again.

"Pauline?" Bill yelled. "What the fuck is this?"

"After all this, you're still going," Pauline said. "The worst fuckers always do survive, ey."

Pat's eyes went wide as Bill spat something furious and strode across the cave. He seemed to be entirely oblivious of the monster in their midst, making his way directly to Pauline.

Kealan and Pat sidled around the other way.

"Get between it and the women," Pat said. "Maybe we can use gunfire to hold it back and get them past us."

"I think Pauline is trapped there."

They came up beside Sheila and her eyes were cinched in pain and sadness. Bill found himself suddenly alone with the roo in the middle of the cave, the rest huddled around Pauline.

"What the fuck, you lot?" he demanded, then remembered himself and spun to face the monster. He brought his shotgun up and fired, the blast enough to make their ears sing. The roo's chest took the full impact, point blank, and a searing jet of flame burst out. It hit Bill and he staggered backwards, arms up to protect himself, hair and eyebrows scorched away. He came up against the stone wall of the cave and looked in horror as the roo leaned onto its front paws and swing its big back legs through, closing the gap between them.

Bill raised the shottie again, but the roo grabbed the barrels and bent them up, ripping the weapon from Bill's hands. He began to scream and shout as the monster leaned on its thick tail and pedalled both huge back feet rapidly. Its two long central claws ripped into

Bill, shredded the skin from his face, tore the clothes and flesh from his chest and stomach. His torso split open, organs tumbling out to be kicked and flipped around as the roo kept battering the man at a furious pace. Blood erupted from his mouth, arms spasming out to either side as he was shredded where he stood. He was long dead, and would have dropped if the roo's frantic kicking didn't keep him up, splattering his blood and bones up the cave wall.

"That's all I wanted," Pauline said quietly.

"We have to get her out of here," Pat said.

Sheila pointed to the massive beam holding Pauline trapped. "We can't lift it! Maybe all of us, together?"

They turned their attention to the wood as the roo let Bill Catter drop and turned to face them.

"You can't kill it, can you?" Pauline said.

"No," Pat grunted, struggling with the beam. "Guns, running it down, nothing works." He briefly remembered Jim McLeod and his dynamite and wondered if they would survive long enough to get back to town and try to do something with that.

"It's me," Pauline said.

"What?"

"It's killing everyone, indiscriminate, but keeping me alive, right? Keeping me safe down here."

The roo hopped over and grasped Kealan by the shoulders. The man yelped and tried to shoot back over his shoulder as it dragged him backwards.

"It's me," Pauline said again. "I summoned it. I'm keeping it here." She looked hard at Sheila. "Kill me."

"Pauline, no," Pat said, but Sheila took the rifle from where he'd leaned it against the wall.

"Sheila, what are you doing?"

"I'm so sorry," Pauline said to Sheila.

Sheila nodded. "Me too, darling." She leaned

forward and kissed Pauline's forehead. Pauline nodded, smiled.

Kealan howled in pain as the roo's claws began to carve into his shoulders.

"We all deserve better, you especially," Sheila said, and put the rifle barrel up under Pauline's chin.

"Thank you," Pauline said, and pushed her head forward.

Tears streamed over Sheila's cheeks as she pulled the trigger. Pauline's head exploded up and back and her body hung instantly limp. As her blood poured down the wood, the roo let out a bellow of anguish.

It dropped Kealan, who writhed in pain on the dirt, blood soaking the shoulders of his shirt. Pat grabbed his leg and dragged him over as the roo began to shudder, shaking more and more violently. It stretched up, stood on its sharp-clawed toes, its head brushing the stone above, and roared again. Its mouth opened impossibly wide, fire shot out bathing the cave in a bright orange glow. Flames jetted from its eyes and it shook more violently still, then began to fold in on itself. A distant howl, that seemed to come from all around them and from an impossible distance at the same time, echoed as the beast shrank down. Then with a final incandescent burst of light and a blast of sulphurous stench, it fell to the ground.

As their eyes adjusted to the seemingly pale white glow of the various phone lights, all they saw on the cave floor was a skinny, ragged male red kangaroo, not even full grown. Its mouth was a bloody mess, chips of broken fangs scattered around it. Its throat was cut, dried blood around the wound like horrific lipstick. Pat nudged it with the toe of his boot and it shifted loosely then settled back.

"Fuck me dead," he breathed. He turned and

gathered his crying wife into a hug. "That was the strongest thing I've ever seen anyone do," he said quietly.

She buried her head in his neck, sobbing, "Oh, Pat. Poor Pauline. And Sharon!"

He nodded. "And so many others. Jesus Christ, so many."

"Is it over?" Kealan said through clenched teeth, hands pressed to his shoulders.

Pat and Sheila turned and helped him up. "Yeah," Pat said. "I think it is. Come on, let's get outta here. I need a fucken drink."

"Tracy'll have to pour for ya," Kealan said with a crooked grin.

"Fine by me." He put his arm around Kealan's back, Sheila supporting from the other side, and they began to help him out.

"You okay, Sadie?" Sheila asked back over her shoulder.

"Yeah. Thanks. I'm okay. Coming."

Sadie stared at the large leather-bound book on the old steamer trunk. She looked up, watched the three retreating backs for a moment. Then she picked up the book, closed it, and tucked it into the back of her shorts, lifting her shirt over to cover it. With a self-satisfied smile, she hurried after the others, heading back out into the daylight.

END

Read more from Alan Baxter
https://www.alanbaxteronline.com/books/

AFTERWORD

I hope you enjoyed all that blood-soaked gonzo mayhem. But no monster story is really just about the monster. I'm not here to preach, I just want to tell fun stories, yet all stories are lies which contain truths. Domestic violence is a massive problem, everywhere in the world, and especially in Australia. The links between domestic violence, particularly violence against women, and greater acts of domestic terrorism are well-established. DV and male suicide are particularly prevalent in country areas in Australia. Men, we need to be better. We need to feel our emotions, learn how to cry, how to ask for help and how to look out for each other. We need to bring our sons up to be better than we are.

GLOSSARY

Throughout this novella, I've used Australian English spelling, and a large amount of Aussie slang. Hopefully this will help you decipher some of it.

Akubra – a brand of hat, very popular in the country.

arvo – shorthand slang for afternoon.

back of beyond – a long way from anything.

blowie – a blow job.

bull bar – a device installed on the front of a vehicle to protect its front from collisions, whether accidental collision with a large animal on rural roads, or intentional collision with another vehicle, such as in police use.

blue – a fight or argument.

cactus – dead, or useless/broken.

chinwag – a conversation.

chook – chicken.

come a cropper – to fail or suffer a defeat; to be struck by misfortune; to literally fall, for example, from a horse.

dunny – a toilet, especially an old-fashioned outdoor toilet in a small shed.

galah – slang for a fool or idiot, actually the name of the grey-backed, pink-breasted cockatoo. The word comes from the Yuwaalaraay and related Aboriginal languages of northern New South Wales.

get a dog up ya – go fuck yourself.

IGA – Independent Grocers of Australia, a franchise chain of independently owned supermarkets.

mad as a cut snake – very angry or crazy.

ocker – characteristically Australian; uncouth, uncultured, or aggressively boorish in a stereotypically Australian manner.

raw prawn – "Don't you come the raw prawn with me" – to treat like a fool or try to deceive (a raw prawn is a hard thing to swallow).

rollie – roll-up, a handmade cigarette.

root – other than the underneath parts of a plant, it also means to fuck.

root your boot – go fuck your boot.

sanger – sandwich.

a few sangers short of a picnic – not all there in the brains department.

schooner – a beer glass, 425 ml (15 imp fl oz), or three-quarters of an imperial pint pre-metrication.

shag – a fuck.

strewth – expression of surprise or dismay, from "God's truth!"

Strine – the English language as spoken by Australians; the Australian accent, especially when considered pronounced or uneducated.

strop – in a strop – in an angry mood; annoyed.

thongs – flip-flops, the footwear. Thong as underwear is a G-string in Aus.

toey – touchy and quick to anger; nervous or anxious. (Can also be used for someone eager for sexual activity or aroused).

ute – a pick-up truck, short for utility vehicle.

we're not here to fuck spiders – we're not here to waste time.

yakka – hard work.

yeah nah – no (similarly "nah yeah" means yes).

your blood's worth bottling – you're a lovely person.

ABOUT ALAN BAXTER

Alan Baxter is a multi-award-winning British-Australian author of horror, supernatural thrillers, and dark fantasy. He's also a martial arts expert, a whisky-soaked swear monkey, and dog lover. He creates dark, weird stories among dairy paddocks on the beautiful south coast of NSW, Australia, where he lives with his wife, son, and hound. The author of nearly twenty books including novels, novellas, and two short story collections, so far, you can find him online at www.warriorscribe.com or on Twitter @AlanBaxter and Facebook. Feel free to tell him what you think. About anything.